NO PLACE FOR VENGEANCE

(MURDER IN THE KEYS: BOOK #3)

JADEN SKYE

Books by Jaden Skye

THE CARIBBEAN MURDER SERIES
DEATH BY HONEYMOON (Book #1)
DEATH BY DIVORCE (Book #2)
DEATH BY MARRIAGE (Book #3)
DEATH BY DESIRE (Book #4)
DEATH BY DECEIT (Book #5)
DEATH BY JEALOUSY (Book #6)
DEATH BY PROPOSAL (Book #7)
DEATH BY OBSESSION (Book #8)
DEATH BY DEVOTION (Book #9)
DEATH BY BETRAYAL (Book #10)
DEATH BY REQUEST (Book #11)
DEATH BY ENGAGEMENT (Book #12)
DEATH BY SEDUCTION (Book #13)
DEATH BY TEMPTATION (Book #14)
DEATH BY INVITATION (Book #15)
DEATH BY WEDDING (Book #16)

THE TOM'S RIVER SAGA
A PERFECT STRANGER (Book #1)

MURDER IN THE KEYS
NO PLACE TO DIE (Book #1)
NO PLACE TO VANISH (Book #2)
NO PLACE FOR VENGEANCE (Book #3)
NO PLACE FOR MARRIAGE (Book #4)

THE KILLING GAME
INVITATION TO DIE (Book #1)
INVITATION TO MADNESS (Book #2)
INVITATION TO AGONY (Book #3)

ISBN: 978-1-64029-181-2

CHAPTER ONE

Olivia stood proudly at her graduation ceremony, palms sweating, eager to receive her license as a certified private detective. After six months of intensive training, she could hardly believe she was done, ready to go out into the world. The training had been a whirlwind experience. She'd learned how to shoot, become an expert in self-defense, and learned how to ruthlessly track down a criminal.

Standing here at the ceremony in Florida, Olivia smiled broadly. The day was sunny, clear, and breezy. Dressed in a crisp linen suit, in her early thirties with her long, blonde hair around her shoulders, Olivia felt on top of the world. Who would have ever thought it would have come to this? Just half a year ago, she'd had a cushy job in publishing in Manhattan and was about to become engaged to Todd. Now she stood here ruggedly, on her own, about to embark on an entirely new phase of her life. This had been totally unplanned and unexpected—and yet it felt completely right.

Olivia's mother and twin sister had been horrified when they'd learned what she planned to do. They complained about it constantly, but there was no way they could stop her. Her father, Blake, had been somewhat more accepting. He must have realized that Todd's sudden murder in Key West, right after their engagement, had been traumatic for Olivia and that was what had prompted her decision.

"Olivia Wells." As the head of the program called out her name, she walked up to receive both her certificate and her license to carry. Olivia heard scattered applause in the room as she accepted the papers proudly and walked back to her seat.

"You've all done wonderfully," he went on, after all the certificates had been handed out. "You are now embarking upon important work, helping to maintain order and justice in a world that has gone awry."

Scattered applause rang out again. Olivia bowed her head briefly. She knew one thing for certain: her own personal world had definitely gone awry, and she desperately needed to set it straight once again.

After the ceremony, Olivia went back to her new apartment in Key West. It was large and airy, on the first floor of a small apartment building in the center of town, and Olivia planned to use half of the apartment to live in, and the other half as the office for her newly formed company: *Olivia Wells Private Investigations*.

Her apartment had two separate entrances. One led directly to the office, the other to Olivia's personal quarters. Although the building was easily accessible to the public, it was also next to a gaggle of trees and ponds. Fortunately, Olivia's personal quarters overlooked the trees and ponds. It was a unique arrangement and Olivia was grateful for it.

As soon as she arrived home, Olivia promptly hung the shingle she'd prepared on the front door. *Olivia Wells, Private Investigator* was boldly engraved on the wooden plank for all the world to see.

Olivia took a step back and smiled as she looked at it. The shingle lifted her spirits but also made her nervous at the same time. Was she being presumptuous to undertake this alone? She'd find out soon enough, she thought.

Olivia walked inside to her personal quarters and opened the door to the main sitting room. The wicker sofa she'd just purchased a few days before stood happily against the far wall. Upholstered in a beautiful, colorful pattern, it was also comfortable to sit in. Above the sofa hung photos of Olivia and Todd. They would serve as a reminder of what had happened, she thought, and keep her motivated when she hit rough sailing.

The rest of the apartment was decorated simply, with plants, a few side chairs, and lightweight tables and lamps. The bedroom had a cheerful yellow, flowered bedspread and pillows, with photos of friends and family on display. It would only be a matter of time, Olivia thought, before the place would really feel like home.

Olivia sat down on a chair across from the couch and looked up at the photos of her and Todd. It was almost as if he were here with her now, keeping an eye on everything. Since Todd's death Olivia's life had been a whirlwind. Not only had she been responsible for solving his murder, but she'd attracted lots of attention in the news. After that, Olivia had returned briefly to Manhattan but couldn't stay in her apartment or job any longer. Fortunately, a call quickly came to come back down to Florida to work on a new case.

After Olivia had solved the second case, her name was blasted over the news once again. People began contacting her. Realizing how much she enjoyed the work, Olivia decided to train to do this work thoroughly and professionally. She'd also decided to move down to Key West.

Olivia stared at the photo of Todd. To her surprise the usual lurch of pain she felt when she looked at it wasn't there any longer. Both the passage of time and her decision to throw herself completely into a new direction had eased her feelings.

Olivia got up and walked into the section of the apartment designated as her office. That room was larger and more formal. A big wooden desk stood in the center with chairs across from it. On the walls were photos of sailboats, the ocean, sunsets, and other pictures of Key West.

Olivia walked over to her desk gingerly, ran her hands across the top of it, and wondered. Would this really work? During the months she'd been in training, she hadn't been in the public eye. Would anyone actually call and hire her to work on a case? She'd put an announcement about the opening of her business in the papers and online. But no one had contacted her. By now, Olivia had friends and acquaintances in the police department down in Key West, but she hadn't heard from them, either.

Olivia sat at her desk, feeling engulfed at the silence. She checked her email and her voicemail: nothing.

She stared at her desk phone, willing it to ring, willing someone to contact her.

But all that came was a deep silence. She sat there, staring at it, and could hear her clock tick.

Would this really work? She only had so much money left, and if it didn't, she'd have to return home—the last thing she wanted to do.

Olivia finally stood, needing to get out of the office. She decided to go for a walk on the charming, winding streets of Key West she'd grown to love.

Anything to take her mind off of her worry for her future.

*

The afternoon was balmy with a soft breeze blowing and Olivia walked slowly, stopping at one shop and then another, gazing at their wares. She looked at handmade jewelry, pottery, tie-dyed shirts and scarves and flowing dresses. Olivia enjoyed the naturalness and ease of Key West and easily smiled and chatted with all the different kinds of people who were working in the stores.

3

As she walked out of a shop, Olivia suddenly heard her name being called.

"Is that you, Olivia?" a male voice sounded behind her.

Olivia turned around. To her complete surprise, there stood Wayne, a detective on the police force. He was dressed in khaki pants and an open, blue shirt, with his sandy hair ruffled as usual. Wayne had worked closely with Olivia when Todd had been killed and helped with her second case as well.

"Wayne?" Olivia was delighted.

He smiled broadly.

"I've been wondering how you've been doing," he said. "I heard over the grapevine that you were taking PI training."

Olivia smiled. What grapevine was that? She had no idea anyone knew about it.

"That's right," she said cheerfully. "In fact, I've just gotten my license."

He beamed. "Why didn't you tell me?"

Olivia had actually been avoiding Wayne after moving down here. She needed time by herself to recover from Todd's death. If Todd's sudden death had taught her anything, it was how important it was to be able to stand on your own.

Time had passed now, though, and it was fun seeing Wayne again.

She blushed, not knowing what to say.

Wayne softened.

"We have to celebrate," he said.

That surprised her. She thought he'd be angry with her. And Olivia felt surprisingly relaxed being with him. She smiled.

"Let's grab a cup of coffee, and toast to the occasion." He grinned boyishly.Actually, the timing couldn't be more perfect, Olivia thought. Her whole life, she had always said no, had kept her guard up. Maybe now was a time to say yes. To take a chance.

"I'd love it," she replied.

Wayne turned toward the outdoor café at the end of the block. "How's that?" he asked.

"Let's go," she said.

As they walked side by side to the corner it felt as though no time had passed since they'd seen each other. The café on the corner was mostly empty at this hour, and Wayne and Olivia got seats outside under the huge palm tree that overhung that spot. Tiny birds flew in and out of the branches as they sat down.

Wayne ordered two cappuccinos and they looked at each other for a long moment. Olivia enjoyed the light breeze blowing on her face.

"You look wonderful," he said.

"Thank you," she said. "So do you."

"You've come a long way since last time I saw you," Wayne continued. "And now you're a licensed private investigator, to boot."

"If I'm going to do this work, I have to do it right."

"Yes, you do," Wayne agreed. "It definitely can be tricky. But it's a big commitment. What made you decide to go all the way?"

"Todd," said Olivia. "Something like that changes you forever."

He fell quiet.

"It absolutely does," Wayne agreed.

"I can't go back to being the person I was," she said. "So I decided, if I can't go back,

I may as well go forward. There's not much else I can do now, anyway. This work is holding me in its grip."

Wayne nodded thoughtfully. "It's like that for many of us," he said softly as waiter brought their cappuccinos.

Olivia raised the warm, sweet beverage to her mouth and savored it slowly.

"Where do you live now?" Wayne asked, curiously. "Where exactly did you hang your shingle?"

Olivia realized how out of touch she'd been. "Right here in Key West, a few blocks away!"

"Really?" Wayne was startled. "You've moved down here for good?"

"For now," said Olivia.

Wayne seemed to take it all in.

"What kind of cases are you looking for now?" he went on.

"I'll take whatever comes along," said Olivia.

"Good attitude," Wayne replied.

"How are you doing, Wayne?" Olivia asked.

"Same as usual," he answered. "Working hard. More and more involved with restorative justice programs, too."

Olivia remembered that restorative justice had been a long-term interest of Wayne's. She wondered who the people he met were, also wanted to meet them.

"I'd like to tell you more about it someday," Wayne commented.

"I'd love to hear about it," Olivia answered.

5

Wayne drank his full cup of cappuccino quickly then and stood to leave. "Unfortunately, I have to run now to an appointment, though. How about making a date for dinner tonight, so we can really get into details?"

She was about to answer, when suddenly her phone rang.

"Olivia Wells?" a male voice on the other end boomed harshly.

"Yes?" asked Olivia.

"This is Chief of Police Mike Frande from the Key Largo Department," he continued. "I don't know if you've heard yet about what's going on here?"

"No I haven't," breathed Olivia.

Wayne gestured to her that he had to run but would be in touch, and she waved back to him. She felt bad not having a chance to finish their conversation, but this call was too important.

"It's all over the news," the chief replied.

"What is?"

"We've got a missing person case and need all the help we can get. A young woman just disappeared during a tour deep into the Everglades. There's not a second to waste."

Olivia breathed sharply. "The Everglades?"

"She and her husband were staying at a hotel in Key Largo, celebrating their anniversary. We're calling you because we've heard about your work down here with missing persons. We'd like to hire you. Can you come up right away? We'll get a room in a hotel in Key Largo for you and discuss other arrangements when you arrive."

Olivia was elated to have her first job. Yet also worried for the missing girl.

"I'll leave immediately," replied Olivia, her heart beating fast.

"Good." His voice grew more forceful. "We'll be waiting for you."

CHAPTER TWO

Olivia hurried back to her apartment. A case already—she couldn't believe it. How had this happened so fast?

She dashed into her bedroom, yanked her suitcase out of the closet, and opened one bureau drawer after another. Then she tossed what she needed into the suitcase. For a moment she stopped, thought about the case, and shuddered. A young woman was missing in the Everglades! How could anyone possibly survive in a place like that for long?

Olivia grabbed her suitcase and flew outside to her car, which was waiting in the parking lot behind her building. She had to get there immediately.

The drive up to Key Largo would take about two hours, Olivia thought, as she made her way to Overseas Highway One. The highway, one of the world's great scenic drives, went from Key West straight up to Key Largo. It was the best way to go. Known as the magic carpet, it ran along Florida's mainland and crossed endless coral and limestone islets through the various Keys. The highway also crossed many bridges along the way, which connected one gorgeous island with the next.

As soon as she got onto the highway, Olivia was once again awed by the beauty of the place. The incredible sky stretched above her was fleeced with late afternoon clouds. The sea, on her side, alternated from turquoise to blue and then deep green as she drove along. It was even possible she would see one of the dramatic sunsets, where a giant red ball of sun plummeted into the blue water, sending pink, orange, and purple streaks up across the evening sky.

As Olivia drove along it struck her that somewhere, caught in the fantastic lushness of the islands, nature had turned dangerous. A woman was struggling for her life.

The weather was unusually warm and humid for so late in the afternoon, but Olivia reminded herself that this was to be expected in July. She opened the car windows, letting the warm but beautiful breezes from the ocean come in. Olivia wondered about the young woman who had gone missing. Who was she? What happened? She and her husband had come down to Key Largo to celebrate their anniversary. Was he with her on the tour? How could he have let this happen?

Olivia turned on the radio then to hear any more news that might be available. Most of the stations were playing different kinds of music, pop, soft jazz, and even country. Olivia turned to the station playing jazz and waited for a news break. It didn't take long. In a few minutes, the announcer came on, at first warning about the extremely humid weather conditions.

"The stifling heat is to be expected down in the Keys at this time of year," he reported. "But the infestation of insects and mosquitoes down in the glades is worse this year than usual."

Olivia shuddered. She'd had a long-term aversion to bugs of all kinds. Time to get over it fast, she thought.

The announcer continued describing sailing conditions, the winds over the water, and then switched to other news abruptly.

"A full-out search is going on for the woman missing in the glades," he went on. "Police are doing all they can and volunteers are still needed. If you can give a hand, call the police in your location. The young woman has never been down here before, doesn't know the territory. And the gators are out in full profusion. It's possible to survive this, of course, but unlikely."

Olivia momentarily felt faint. The thought of the gators swarming around the victim filled her with horror.

Olivia put her foot on the pedal. She would do all she could, for sure.

Olivia drove on pointedly, remembering her brief meeting with the Key Largo police during her last case here. She was surprised that they'd reached out to her now, didn't realize she'd made an impression upon them. Last time she was here was different, though. She'd been here with Wayne, the Key West police force, and other private investigators who'd been hired. Now she was arriving on her own. Olivia was eager to hear what more the police could tell her.

As the light of the day faded, her car made its way up through the exquisite islands to Key Largo. The moment she arrived there, Olivia quickly pulled off the highway and slowly entered the sprawling town.

*

It was good to be back in Key Largo once again. Although the island didn't have the glamour, fascination, or culture of Key West, Olivia liked it. A total of about thirty miles, Key Largo was the longest of the group of islands in the Florida Keys. It was an extremely popular diving resort and attracted divers the world over. With many reefs and areas of natural beauty around its shores, Key Largo also offered the best scuba diving and snorkeling. The many national parks offered a chance to hike, bike, kayak, and more. But the most fascinating part was that Key Largo was also in easy reach of the Everglades National Park. Daring tourists could come down here and go on all kinds of incredible tours, see parts of the Everglades few people ever see or venture into.

The police station wasn't far from the highway, only a few blocks down the center of town. Olivia pulled up at the station and parked. She got out of the car, straightened her lime summer dress, tossed her long, blonde hair off her face, and walked right to the main entrance.

As soon as she entered, Olivia saw a tall, young officer was seated at the front door.

"Olivia Wells?" the officer asked, almost as if he were waiting for her.

"Yes," said Olivia, relieved that she was being greeted.

The officer stood up quickly. He was slender, toned, and energetic, with short dark hair and no-nonsense dark eyes.

"Officer Weston Garland," he introduced himself and held out his hand.

Olivia shook his hand briefly. "Thanks for waiting for me."

"My pleasure." Weston smiled, looking a bit taken aback by Olivia. "The guys will be pleased you got here so fast."

Olivia nodded as Weston led her down the hallway to the main meeting room at the end. As she walked inside, a group of officers stood up to greet her. A large, heavier officer stepped in front immediately.

"Chief of Police Mike Frande," he announced. "Pleased to have you with us, Olivia."

"Thank you," Olivia replied as he motioned for her and the others to sit down.

"Your reputation precedes you," he added. "And you lost no time in getting here. That's good."

Mike Frande then walked to the long table in front of the room and pointed to a screen that stood beside it. "We have no time to lose so I'm going to start right away and give you an overview of what we're up against. I'll show you some slides of the woman who's gone missing and the area where she was last seen."

Pictures of lush, wild greenery, trees, birds, insects, and swamps came up on the screen. "The Everglades is a rich and complicated place," Mike started. "This is a wildlife preserve, filled with untamed and dangerous creatures, and filled with winding, swampy trails."

Olivia was mesmerized by the wild, shocking beauty she was looking at.

Next, a large photo of a beautiful young couple flashed on the screen. The young woman had long, auburn hair and the man was blond and stately. They looked well suited, happy and smiling.

"This is Amanda, who's gone missing. Next to her stands her husband, Tye Fisher," Mike continued. "The couple came down here to Key Largo to celebrate their anniversary. They live in Connecticut. Amanda teaches music at a private high school, and he's a rather successful, established architect."

"They're interesting," Olivia murmured. Not exactly the kind of couple she'd imagine would come to the Everglades.

"Yes, they are," Mike continued. "Our research on them has turned up nothing out of the ordinary. A young, happy, successful couple. They have friends who speak well of them and their relationship."

"Was the husband with the wife on the tour?" Olivia asked immediately.

Mike stopped speaking a moment as Weston smiled crisply.

"Good question," said Weston. "No, he wasn't."

Olivia was startled to hear that. "Why not?"

"Have you heard anything about the case at all?" Mike interrupted.

"Just a few words on the car radio driving up here," Olivia replied. "You have a hotline set up already, I imagine?"

"A hotline is putting it mildly," said Weston. "And we're flooded with all kinds of bizarre tips, too. It's par for the course. Nothing unusual. We're getting sightings of Amanda as far as Alabama. Most of them are nonsense, of course. But everyone wants to be part of the action."

"That's the problem with hotlines," Mike added. "It takes thousands of hours to track the calls down and most of them are bogus. But back to the main point for a minute. You asked why Amanda's husband didn't accompany her on the tour in the Everglades. It is a good question. Tye told us that he woke up feeling ill that morning. He wasn't up to taking a trip like that. He even asked Amanda to postpone it a few days, but she refused. He said she was determined to go that day."

Olivia listened carefully. "Is he telling the truth?"

"We've grilled him thoroughly," Weston broke in now. "But we want you to speak to him yourself, alone, at his hotel nearby. A woman's touch could help soften him up in case he's got more information. We've been the bad cop in the case, you can be the good one!"

Olivia smiled. Weston was tough and blunt, but his directness was refreshing.

"I'd be happy to be the good cop," Olivia replied.

"Go give the guy some cookies and tea," another officer, who had introduced himself as Tommy, chimed in.

"Tye must be terrified," Olivia said.

"I wouldn't call it terrified, exactly," Weston replied. "Actually, he seems confident that Amanda's well and we'll find her."

That seemed odd to Olivia. Why would he be so confident?

"No, Olivia's right. The husband's terrified," Mike's voice boomed loudly. "How could he not be? The guy's holding it together as best he can."

"It's almost like he's used to trouble with her," Weston added.

Olivia found that extremely interesting. "If he's used to trouble with her, do you think he's complicit in her disappearance?" She wasn't pulling any punches. Usually spouses were the first persons of interest.

"What do you mean complicit?" Mike retorted. "You mean do we think he's guilty?"

"Do you?" asked Olivia.

"Guilty of what?" Tommy burst in. "His wife's missing. She isn't dead. Nobody has any idea what happened to her."

"The tour set out early in the morning," Weston continued. "Amanda went missing at five thirty p.m. Tye was seen at his hotel at five o'clock. He went downstairs to the restaurant at that time and had something to eat. His alibi checks out. Others saw him there, too."

"Who the hell knows what it means though?" Tommy burst in again, rubbing his big jowls. "I don't put much stock in alibis. Why in hell was the husband down at the restaurant so close to the time she went missing? To set himself up as innocent?"

Olivia shivered. Tommy was tough and seasoned, nobody's fool.

Tommy turned to Olivia then. "You can't take anything for granted in a case like this. You've got to figure every single angle."

"Of course," agreed Olivia.

"We also talked to the main tour guide, Jack Healey, who runs the tour company Amanda was on. It's an established company, very reliable," Weston jumped in. "The tour went through alligator swamps. When they stopped for a break and were about to turn back, Amanda wanted to go on, past the place the guide said was safe. She insisted she was an experienced hiker. They told her it wasn't a good idea. There was fifteen minutes downtime and the tour was then set to return."

"What happened then?" asked Olivia, transfixed.

"Amanda decided to separate from the tour and hike further on her own. She said she would just be gone for ten minutes or less. They told her that she'd have to take the risk on her own. She said she'd take the risk, and set off. After half an hour she didn't come back. When forty-five minutes passed, everyone started looking for her. No sign of anything. They called the news into the cops after an hour."

"People on the tour were the last to see her alive then?" Olivia exclaimed.

"Sure, who else?" Mike looked at Olivia strangely. "If there was someone else, we sure need to hear about them."

Olivia was enrapt. Why would Amanda separate from the tour and go on her own into a life-threatening situation? It didn't make sense. And how could it be that she disappeared completely, with no sign of her at all? All ghastly possibilities stirred in Olivia's mind.

"The alligators?" Olivia started.

Tommy spun around and looked at her squarely. "Were the gators hungry? Of course. Did Amanda get caught by one of them, or more? We sure as hell hope not." Tommy gave voice to Olivia's silent questions.

"How else could there be no sign of her, no remains, not anything?" Olivia replied.

"That's the question, isn't it?" Weston chimed in.

"The gators could have gotten her, but not likely," Mike joined the conversation.

"Why not?" asked Olivia.

"The trails around the swamp are well carved out. It wasn't a night tour. There was still enough light left for her to see where she was going."

"No one on the tour went onwards with her, though?" Olivia needed to be sure about every single detail.

"Not that we heard of," said Mike. "We've talked to Jack, and most of the passengers on the tour. There's one left."

"That's important," said Olivia.

"Of course it is. We're well aware of that. This all just broke. One thing at a time," Mike replied.

"Clearly you didn't find cause to bring Jack in for further questioning?" Olivia had to be certain.

"Clearly we didn't." Mike suddenly seemed to be growing exasperated. "If we had, he would be here at the station, right now. Jack Healey's tours are well known. He has a fine reputation."

"We have to trace that other passenger down right away, though," Weston added. "Could be he's traumatized and doesn't want to speak to anyone right this second."

"He has to anyway," Tommy grumbled. "To hell with his trauma! Amanda's got more trauma than him right now."

"If she's still alive," Weston added slowly.

A moment of silence filled the room. Olivia couldn't entertain the idea that Amanda was dead. She had to hold onto hope and talk to every single person involved. She also had to learn more about the glades as well, go there herself. It was crucial to get a firsthand sense of where Amanda had been when she'd disappeared.

"At this moment, what are your conclusions and plans?" Olivia asked Mike directly.

"No conclusions yet," Mike quickly engaged. "It's way too early for that. First we need to find out a lot more about Amanda and also her husband. That's where you come in. There are tricky characters down here in these parts. There could be hidden motives for what happened. For all we know others are involved in her disappearance. Before we say she came to harm from the gators, everything else has to be ruled out."

"Of course," Olivia agreed.

"We need to uncover everything about her. Secrets you could never dream of. People don't go on tours and just disappear," Mike went on.

"Unless they purposely want to end their lives?" Tommy speculated.

"Or unless somebody else wanted to end it," Weston echoed.

"Until we get some answers, this will look bad for tourism in the Everglades," Tommy added. "It's how they make a living and keep the preserve in good shape."

"I understand," said Olivia.

"Good," Weston shot back. "So the next step is, you talk to Amanda's husband at his hotel nearby. Find out if he'll tell you anything he hasn't told us."

He peered at her.

"And find out if he's hiding anything."

CHAPTER THREE

Olivia drove a couple of blocks and checked in to her hotel room. The room was large and airy with a good view of the sky. Fortunately, it looked out above over the other buildings around and a few evening stars could even be seen. Olivia threw her bag down on the small sofa and sat down to catch her breath. She realized how hectic the next days were about to become. She put her stuff down and was preparing to leave again when her cell rang.

"Sorry to rush out of the café." Wayne was on the other end. "There was a little emergency here and I got caught up. But I didn't forget our date for dinner."

Olivia was startled to hear his voice. In all the excitement, she'd completely forgotten their dinner appointment. "Oh my goodness," she breathed.

"Is it too late now? Should we try for tomorrow?" Wayne continued.

"Wayne, I'm in Key Largo now," Olivia breathed. "I'm so sorry, dinner skipped my mind."

"Key Largo?" Wayne sounded taken aback.

"It all happened so fast. I got the call right after I saw you, and immediately came running up here," Olivia explained.

"Are you on the case of the woman who went missing in the glades?" Wayne was enthralled.

"Yes," Olivia whispered. "The call came in from the Key Largo police."

"My God," said Wayne.

"I know," said Olivia, "I'm in my hotel room now. I went to the station first and they filled me in on all kinds of details."

"You're working Mike Frande?" Wayne continued. "I know him well. Mike's a terrific cop."

"I am working with him and also a few others on the force," Olivia replied. "They all seem good."

"This is big time, Olivia." Wayne was impressed. "It's tricky too, be careful."

"I will be careful." Olivia smiled. "I'm trained for this now."

"Your training has just started," Wayne replied quickly. "Each new case is training,"

15

Olivia realized he was looking after her. "Listen, we'll definitely catch up later on," she said. "I'll take a rain check for that dinner."

"You got it," Wayne replied. "And please, keep me informed. If I can help in any way, I'd like to."

"Thanks, Wayne," said Olivia. "That means a lot."

"Of course," he replied. "I'm just a phone call away."

*

Olivia checked herself in the car mirror. Her clear blue eyes looked back at her. She looked different than she had a few days ago, stronger, more centered. She looked like someone who knew just where she was, and what she was doing.

The drive to Tye's hotel took about five minutes. Tye was up in his room, waiting for Olivia, not wanting to be downstairs in public right now.

Olivia went right to his room and knocked on the door. In less than a second, it flung open and Tye stood there dressed in jeans and an expensive yellow summer shirt. Just as in the picture she'd seen of him on the slide show, Tye was blond and handsome with a regal air about him. And, despite his excessively calm exterior, Olivia noticed one of his hands trembling at his side.

Tye stood there stiffly now, looking at Olivia carefully before speaking. "Come in, please," he said finally "You're young to be doing this kind of work, aren't you? Not at all what I expected."

Olivia didn't feel the need to prove herself at all, just walked into the room and looked around. His hotel room was elegant, uncluttered, and in strangely perfect order. It was hard to imagine anyone even occupying it.

Tye stepped in front of Olivia then, taking charge. He pointed to an emerald green chair. "Please sit down here," he said, "and we can talk further."

"I'm terribly sorry for what you're going through," Olivia started, as she sat down.

Tye sat opposite her and said nothing for a moment.

"This must be extremely frightening to you," she went on.

"It could be, if I let it," he answered coolly. "I can't let it though. I have to keep calm and clear-eyed, don't I?"

"Yes, you do," said Olivia, agreeing fully.

"I've spoken to the police already and I suppose I have to go through it all again with you now," he continued.

16

"It's helpful to go through what happened with different people," answered Olivia. "Everyone sees something others haven't."

Tye bit his lip and shook his head. "Okay, here goes. Amanda and I have been married for a year. This is our first anniversary and we came to Key Largo to celebrate."

"Did you both plan to take a tour of the glades as part of the celebration?" Olivia was curious. Tye didn't seem like someone who would celebrate in that manner.

"Yes, that was part of the plan," he answered nondescriptly. "Amanda loves extreme sports and adventures. She planned the outing. I agreed to it."

"Did you want to go, though?" Olivia was fascinated.

"I wanted to be with her, of course, and make her happy," Tye replied. "She loves a thrill and I knew it when we got married."

"You don't love a thrill?" Olivia asked quietly.

Tye smiled for a brief moment. "Do I look like a daredevil?" he asked.

Olivia smiled as well. "Looks can be deceiving," she replied.

"I assure you I never wanted to explore the Everglades, but I certainly do now," he answered abruptly. "I want to go and find her!"

"Where do you think she is?" Olivia was quick on the draw.

"I think she's alive and hiding somewhere," Tye quickly answered.

"Hiding, why?" Olivia felt uncomfortable.

"That's for us to find out, isn't it?" he responded.

"Was something threatening her, was she in danger?" Olivia asked, feeling chills run up and down her arms.

"Not at all, she was fine, well cared for, happy." Tye smiled oddly.

"Where do you think she might be hiding?" Olivia wouldn't let it go.

"I don't know where, I don't know the terrain, but she's smart, she's careful, she knows what she's doing." Tye spoke with great confidence.

"Do you think your wife ran away on purpose to hide?" Olivia pressed.

"I'm not saying that," Tye quickly answered. "I'm saying if something happened and she got into trouble Amanda would know how to be safe. She'd find a hiding place."

"What kind of trouble are you talking about?" Olivia asked again.

17

"I told you, she's smart, she's agile," Tye repeated, growing nervous.

"Does Amanda know the terrain? Has she been here before?"

"No, she hasn't been here before," he replied, "but she's studied the glades carefully. We have books all around and maps. She's been watching videos about it."

Olivia and Tye looked at each other for a long moment.

"What is she looking for here, Tye?" Olivia asked.

"That's a great question." He seemed impressed. "I believe Amanda's looking for thrills, excitement, a taste of real nature as she calls it. She said she can't live without it."

"That's quite a statement," breathed Olivia.

"Yes, it is," he replied. "She's also given to extreme comments."

"Amanda seems to have a need to break out of the mold," Olivia mused.

Tye stared at Olivia then. "That's putting it mildly," he quipped.

Olivia couldn't help wonder what their marriage was like. Tye seemed like the epitome of someone who fit the mold, did well in it.

"You like that wildness about her?" Olivia went on. "It's like a breath of fresh air to you?"

"To a point, I like it. To a point, only." Tye bristled. "Listen, what's all this got to do with finding my wife and bringing her home?"

"The more I know about your wife, the more we can figure where she is and what happened," Olivia replied.

"I want to go there myself and look," Tye replied. "The police won't let me. They want me to stay put in the hotel. There are plenty of people searching right now. Strangers are coming from all over to find Amanda."

"I heard that," Olivia replied.

"The cops said I could become a target, as well," Tye went on shakily.

"A target for what?"

"Who knows?" He shrugged intensely. "If someone is after her, if someone did something to her on purpose, they could turn on me then, I suppose."

"Does that scenario make sense to you?" Olivia paid close attention to him now. "Is there anyone at all you know of that could wish her ill?"

"No. Not that I know of," Tye replied tartly. "Look, I was supposed to go with her on the tour that morning but woke up feeling unwell. I had a loose stomach and couldn't make it." As he went on Tye grew more agitated. "I asked Amanda to postpone it a day or so, but she wouldn't. She wanted to be on this specific tour into the swamps. We'd booked it awhile ago and it was hard to get on. She said we could take another tour later on, when I was better."

"Once she made up her mind that was that?" Olivia commented.

"You got that right." Tye shook his head slowly.

"Tell me about your marriage, Tye," Olivia continued.

"It's good, it's fine, we're happy," he replied.

"You're very different from each other, though, aren't you?" Olivia had to have more details.

"In some ways we're different," said Tye, "and in others we're the same. We fit well together. It's a good balance overall."

"You've known each other for a long while?"

"We dated for over two years before the wedding," he replied. "Everyone thought we were a wonderful couple. They were thrilled to be at the wedding, happy we'd tied the knot."

Olivia listened carefully. She saw no reason to doubt what he was saying. Tye was certainly believable in every way.

"What a mess," Olivia murmured. "I'm really sorry this happened."

"Thanks," said Tye, getting up off his chair. "Listen, you've got to help me. I'm asking you to do everything you can to find Amanda immediately! I'll make it worth your while."

"It's already worth my while," Olivia breathed. "This is my work. I love it."

"And don't listen to what others are saying," he went on. "Don't give up hope, no matter what they say."

"I never give up hope," Olivia replied. "And I'm going to go myself to the Everglades immediately to find out exactly where she was, and what could have happened there."

CHAPTER FOUR

Key Largo was about a thirty- to forty-minute drive to the entrance of Everglades National Park. Olivia decided that next she had to go and speak to Jack Healey. He was the guide who owned the company Amanda had been on tour with. When Olivia called his office they said she'd find Jack either at the Everglades National Park or in Everglades City. They suggested that she start with the park. Most likely he'd be there. Olivia decided to take their suggestion and start looking for Jack at the Everglades National Park.

Without giving it another moment's thought, she got back into her car and pulled out some maps for directions. She had the option to take the fast four-lane Alligator Alley, or the more scenic two-lane Tamiami Trail. Olivia immediately chose the Tamiami Trail, which ran through the Big Cypress National Preserve where a thick cypress swamp hugged its edges. Olivia wanted to follow the trails similar to the ones Amanda was on, to get a better sense of what she really wanted here.

The Everglades National Park was a one-and a half million acre wetlands preserve on the southern tip of Florida. You could find the leatherback turtle down here, the Florida panther, and West Indian manatee. As she drove along, out of the corner of her eye, Olivia had glimpses of alligators sunning along the waterways. There was also an assortment of huge, magical birds perched both on the land and in the trees. Olivia had to force herself to keep her eyes on the road, not stop and stare at the incredible natural beauty in front of her eyes. This was Florida's version of the wild west, she thought, as she entered the lush and captivating world that was completely set apart from reality.

Olivia drove carefully through sawgrass marshes and pine flatwoods that were home to hundreds of animal species. Even with the car air conditioning on the sweltering heat pressed in through the windows, as little insects of all kinds got stuck on the sweaty windowpane.

Before long, she entered the national park. As she drove along, the ground seemed to be a grassy, slow-moving river made up of coastal mangroves. Olivia didn't know what would turn up next. Fortunately, in a few minutes the Information Center came up on the right.

Olivia parked, got out, and was bowled over by the scalding, thick heat. She quickly rushed inside both to cool off and to find Jack Healey.

A stern-looking woman with short frizzy hair sat up front, underneath large ceiling fans that whirred the hot air around. Dressed in a tight park uniform, the woman looked up the moment Olivia approached.

"What can I do for you?" she asked, not missing a beat.

"I'm here to see Jack Healey," Olivia reported.

"The head of Gliding Tours," the woman announced proudly. "Jack's a fifth-generation guide. You can't find many of those around anymore."

Olivia was duly impressed. "I heard he'd be here now," she went on.

"He was supposed to be, but he's not." The woman bit her lower lip as she swatted a small fly that had landed on her cheek. "Something happened and Jack's still back in Everglades City right now."

Olivia was alerted. "What happened? Something connected to the case?" she quickly asked.

The woman looked nervous. "How do I know? I don't know anything about the case at

all. It's none of my business, is it?"

Olivia looked at her closely. The twang in her tone hit Olivia strangely.

"I'm a private investigator, working with the police on the case down here." Olivia filled the woman in quickly. "If there's anything at all else that you know, I need to hear it right away."The woman got the point. "Okay, there's been all kinds of people coming through our park with one question after another about Amanda," she said. "But she's gone and if you want my opinion the chances are one in a thousand we'll ever see her again."

Olivia felt disturbed. "Why not?"

"Why not?" The woman looked at Olivia as if she were crazy. "Do you know what's living in the swamp?"

For a second Olivia wondered if rabid criminals were also hiding out here.

"These parts are loaded with predators of all kinds," the woman continued. "Take a look. Besides the gators and crocs which call this home, you'll find snakes and critters all over in the roadway.

And Florida panthers are made roadkill every day. They're not exactly friendly, either."

Olivia shivered at the thought of it.

"Amanda could also have had more trouble from dangerous plants too, than any gator or cottonmouth," the woman continued. "Poison ivy, poisonwood, and the miserable manchineel tree with its rotten sap are all over the forests. Too much time has gone by."

"My God," said Olivia, disheartened.

"What do you want to talk to Jack for, anyway?" The woman seemed to have taken a sudden liking to Olivia.

"Jack owned the tour Amanda was on," Olivia replied simply.

The woman frowned. "Okay, so go talk to him. But be careful, it's the hurricane season and we get thunderstorms almost every day now. Temperatures are sweltering, and huge gangs of mosquitoes like to fly together. If they get at you, it can be hell."

Olivia flinched at the thought of it.

"Also, the higher water in summer makes it hard to see hidden wildlife crouched all over. These animals aren't hanging out at the dry season's sloughs. You never know what's hidden right beside you." The woman was being protective of Olivia and she appreciated it.

Olivia wondered for a second why anyone in their right mind would come down here this time of year.

"Why do people come in the summer, anyway?" asked Olivia.

"People come all year long," the woman replied. "Some can't stay away, they're addicted. Once you get the taste for a wild, off the beat place to spot animals in, it's all over. You keep coming back for more. For people who can't stand civilization, this is home."

Olivia suddenly felt cold sober. She could see how the place could be a wild haven from the trials and tribulations of the cold, lonely world many lived in these days.

"Thanks so much for your help," Olivia said to the woman.

"Listen, be careful," the woman replied. "How are you getting over to Everglades City, anyhow?"

"I have a map," Olivia answered.

"There are trails through the glades that can take you there faster," the woman advised. "You'll need to hire a Jeep driver though."

Olivia paused. "Maybe."

"I can get you a Jeep driver to take you. You can leave your car here if you want."

"Thanks, I'll think about it," said Olivia.

The woman grinned. "You're here on business, not on a tour, right?"

"I'm here for both," Olivia replied. She definitely needed to have a similar experience to Amanda's, a tour that would give her a firsthand taste of the territory.

"Be smart, honey," the woman suggested.

"Okay, I'll take the Jeep," Olivia answered boldly.

"Good for you." The woman was surprised. "I'll call my favorite driver right away."

*

Before long Anthony Talin drove his Jeep right up to the entrance of the Information Center, and Olivia climbed in. She was headed to Jack's main office in Everglades City.

"Take good care of her." The woman came outside with Olivia to make sure things went well.

"I take good care of everybody," came Anthony's chuckling reply. "Just fasten yourself in, honey and we'll be there in no time."

The Jeep pulled away immediately and swerved onto a side path down into what seemed like marshes, with huge grass, rocks, and trees all around. Olivia looked out at the endless array of animals crawling around and shivered. The ride was fast and bumpy and she hoped it was safe. At least she would get there quickly, she thought, as loud, odd birds screamed at each other through the tall trees.

Anthony laughed as he drove along. "Not too many know this back road to Everglades City," he said. "I'll get you there in half the time as any other way."

"Great," said Olivia. "Good work." Fortunately, the woman had called ahead for Olivia, said she was on the way. They promised that Jack would be there waiting for her. Olivia definitely needed to get there as fast as possible, and was glad she'd chosen to go by Jeep.

"Hey, look over there." Anthony's large hand flung out of the open window, pointing at a huge alligator creeping along in the road. "You're in his territory now. You've got to respect that."

Olivia gazed at the animal in awe. It was huge, and moved along inch by inch, one with the earth it called home.

"You'll get a good look at everything from Jack's tours, too," Anthony added. "He sure knows how to take his travelers just where they need to go."

Olivia closed her eyes a second as if to visualize where Amanda might be. She wondered where exactly she needed to go. She hadn't expected to be out in the midst of this wilderness so quickly right now. Strangely enough, she felt comfortable in it, not at risk for her life. Anthony and the Jeep gave her a sense of safety. She was close to the animals but far enough away to pay them a visit and move on.

Amanda hadn't been so lucky, though. She hadn't made it home. Whether she realized it or not, she hadn't been safe. Olivia tried to put herself in Amanda's place and imagine what had happened to her when she left her tour and proceeded onward alone. What had driven her to do that? It was still an open question that had to be answered, fast.

CHAPTER FIVE

Jack Healey was a big man, with short hair, warm eyes, and a tense face. The minute Olivia walked into his office, he stood up and greeted her formally.

"Good to see you," he said. "You're a brave young woman coming out here alone."

Olivia never thought of herself as brave. "Thank you for making time to speak to me," she replied.

"Come in and make yourself comfortable," Jack continued.

Olivia walked in and was immediately struck by the many photos hanging all over the walls of Jack's office. His entire life seemed to be on display. First were photos of alligators, crocodiles, panthers, and huge birds alongside the many tourists who had pictures taken with them. Above that you could see photos of the Indians who had once lived in the Everglades. At another side of the wall were shots of what looked like Jack's family members, standing tall together in front of a swamp.

"Quite a collection of photographs you have here," Olivia remarked, "quite a life you've lived. Breathtaking."

Olivia's comment pleased Jack. "You're actually in the presence of a fifth-generation guide," he replied. There are not too many of us left any longer. We have always lived right here in the Everglades, never leave it."

"You never leave the Everglades?" Olivia was stunned.

"No, there's nothing outside of interest," Jack answered. "This place is my home! I am the Everglades. I am one with the glades, part of every winding road and every creature who makes his home here. Our tours are indescribable."

"I can only imagine." Olivia paused, startled by his intensity. "I can barely imagine what it's like to love the place you live so much."

"Not many can," Jack agreed.

"You know why I'm here, of course?" Olivia continued, wanting to get to the point of her visit.

"Naturally," Jack continued. "Inevitably there are occasional tragedies in the glades. They can't be avoided."

That was an odd way to put it, thought Olivia. "There's still hope, though, isn't there?" she asked. "Amanda hasn't been declared dead yet."

Jack looked up at the ceiling briefly, "No, she hasn't," he agreed, "not yet. This young woman went on a rough tour and knew it up front. Her trip went through alligator swamps most never see."

"I heard she was quite an adventurer," said Olivia.

Jack made a sour face. "Amanda was a music teacher in Connecticut," he replied. "People fancy themselves all kinds of things. Call her anything you want, this was the tour she insisted upon. She and her husband booked it quite far in advance. It was a tour for experienced travelers."

"Was she an experienced traveler?" Olivia was fascinated.

"I have no idea," Jack replied nervously. "We don't ask tourists those kinds of questions. There are no qualifications for coming on board. Most people have enough good sense to make the right decisions for themselves. And to be careful!"

"What happened to her?" Olivia asked pointedly, wanting to hear the story from him this time.

"Nobody knows," Jack answered. "And probably they never will."

"Tell me what you know, though," Olivia responded.

"The tour came to a natural resting point, a break, for about fifteen minutes." Jack began reporting the details again. "Amanda wanted to go further, though, past the place we considered safe. There was a hiking trail there, carved out in the middle of the swamps around to its furthest edge. She wanted to walk on it."

"Why?" asked Olivia, incredulous.

"She said she was disappointed that she hadn't seen a Nile crocodile yet, was convinced she'd spot one up ahead a bit. Seems it was a big deal for her to see one."

"Why?" asked Olivia.

"You're asking me questions I can't answer," said Jack, growing agitated. "Different travelers are bent on seeing different sights. Besides that, how do I know what makes a woman tick? It's hard enough figuring my own wife out."

"I mean what are the Nile crocs like?" Olivia corrected herself.

"Nile crocs can grow to eighteen feet long and weigh as much as a small car," Jack continued. "They eat everything, zebras, small hippos, and even humans in sub-Saharan Africa. Recently, they've been spotted swimming in the Everglades and also relaxing on a house porch in Miami. Amanda seemed to have a craving to see one. I suppose she wanted to brag about it to her friends." Jack obviously didn't seem to have much regard for her, or sympathy.

"Is it usual to go hiking in a place like that, looking for such a dangerous creature?" Olivia asked.

"Very unusual, I'd say," Jack retorted. "Of course you get strange ones on some of these tours, even people with suicidal tendencies." He put his head down and then looked up at Olivia confidentially from under his eyes. His comment and glance seemed to suggest that he thought Amanda had taken her own life.

"So far there's no evidence to support the idea that she was depressed or suicidal, though," Olivia responded.

"What kind of evidence are you looking for?" Jack scoffed. "Anyway, this young lady had the right to do what she liked during the break. So, she decided to go forward on her own. No one thought too much about it, either. She said she'd be back in about ten minutes. After forty minutes without her returning, everyone knew something was wrong. The news was called in to the police in about an hour."

"What else was around the area she was hiking in?" Olivia was jarred.

"Besides the alligators, crocodiles, and scattered panthers, nothing, just swamps. And maybe a few huts scattered here and there, on the back roads."

"How far away are the huts?" Olivia hadn't heard about that before.

"Some are all the way at the end of the trail, one is in walking distance. Why?"

"Why?" asked Olivia. "Has anyone been to that hut, looked around?"

"There's only one close by," Jack continued, "and it's an old broken down shack that's always empty. Believe me, no one goes there ever. It's been deserted for years."

Olivia took careful note. "Is this tour Amanda was on given routinely?" She changed the topic slightly.

"Of course," said Jack, "and it's completely safe. The police already asked me that and they also spoke to most of the other passengers on it. Everybody else obeyed the rules and they all came home safe and sound. Until Amanda disappeared, everyone was having a wonderful time."

Olivia took a deep, sad breath. "How far away are the other huts you mentioned in the back?"

"Far enough," he answered. "They're also just ramshackle places, unimportant. From time to time a few fishermen might occupy them. Why?"

"I'm just trying to get a feel for what else could have happened," Olivia said.

"I'm going to leave that to your imagination," Jack grumbled.

"My imagination is not good enough," she answered. "I need facts."

"Well, your imagination has to be good enough, because I have no idea what could have happened, and frankly, no one else does either," Jack snapped. "The county's spending a bloody fortune, too, setting up search teams for her wherever you go."

"That's a good thing," said Olivia.

"I don't spend my time thinking about good or bad," Jack replied. "Things just are what they are here in the Everglades. You go too far where you don't belong, you may not come back."

Olivia took a long, sharp breath. "Did Amanda or her husband ever book a tour with you before?" she asked.

"What has that got to do with anything?" Jack was getting irritated. "I told you all I know. And I told the police the same thing. You're grilling me, honey."

"I have to," Olivia replied. "What about the other people on the tour? Did someone have it in for her? Could they have slipped something to her?"

"That's ridiculous," said Jack, giving Olivia a long, slow glance. "You know when someone comes down here and is out in heat they're not used to, it's possible for them to get paranoid. I've seen it before."

Olivia was put off by his comment. He was suggesting she wasn't in her right mind, trying to put an abrupt end to her questions. But she wasn't going for it.

"Are there any suspects you can think of? Any at all?" Olivia pressed forward.

"If there were I would have told the police, wouldn't I?" Jack briskly replied.

"Did you fight with Amanda, telling her not to go further?" Olivia asked.

Jack grew silent. "Firstly, I never fight with my passengers," he replied. "Secondly, that day someone else was the guide for the last leg of the journey."

"What?" Olivia was stunned. This was the first time she'd heard that. "Who was the guide on her tour when she disappeared?"

"My young cousin Frank," Jack replied. "He lives down here, too, and fills in routinely when he's needed. He's an experienced, terrific guide too."

"I haven't heard about a word about Frank before," breathed Olivia. "Did you mention him to the police?"

"No, I did not," Jack quipped back. "Why should I? What the hell difference does it make? Frank stayed on the boat after she got off it. The other passengers saw him there."

"I need to talk to him anyway." Olivia grew agitated.

"For what reason?" Jack became unsettled now, too.

"Because he was one of the last people to see her alive!"

Jack stood up and turned his back to Olivia for a long moment then. Finally, he turned around again.

"You're making this more complicated than you need to," he said, staring at her.

"Where is Frank? How can we find him?" Olivia would not be put off.

"If it was important to talk to Frank the police would have asked," Jack retorted.

"They don't know he was on the tour so why would they ask?" Olivia was adamant.

"So, call them and tell them," Jack mocked her for a moment.

"I will," said Olivia, "I have to. And I also want you to take me to the exact place where Amanda went missing."

Jack walked to another part of the room then, shaking his head. "This is nuts, really nuts," he mumbled.

Olivia followed after him. "It's my job," she replied. "I can't leave any stone unturned. Right now a young woman's life could be hanging by a thread."

Jack turned around again. "Maybe it is and maybe it isn't," he mumbled. "Go call the police now and see what they say."

"I'll call immediately," said Olivia, "but whatever they say, I want you to take me to see the spot Amanda vanished."

*

Jack stood there tapping his foot on the floor while Olivia immediately put in a call to Mike, the chief of police.

"It's Olivia," she breathed the moment he picked up.

"Hello there, how's it going?" asked Mike.

"I'm here with Jack Healey in Everglades City," Olivia said, "and there's new information."

"What?" Mike's voice grew somber suddenly.

"There was another guide on the water boat Amanda was on when she disappeared. Jack wasn't there then."

"What?" Mike sounded blindsided. "Hold on a minute. Who was this guide?"

"He's a cousin of Jack's, an experienced young man, Frank," Olivia reported.

After a long pause on the other end, Mike breathed heavily. "This is important information. You're good, Olivia. I'll make sure we talk to Frank."

"Good," she replied. "I want to speak to him, too."

"Of course," Mike answered. "What's your next step now?"

"I want to go see the place Amanda disappeared for myself. I just asked Jack to take me," she replied.

"Whoa, hold on a second," Mike broke in. "We don't need a repeat of what just happened to Amanda. There's no knowing what's going on down there. No way you're going alone! It's a good idea to take a look, but I'm sending Weston to join you immediately. Just take a breather and wait for him. He'll be there in no time."

Olivia balked for a moment, but then thought better of it.

"You've got no choice about this one," Mike exclaimed. "I'm calling Jack and telling him not to go anywhere until Weston arrives."

CHAPTER SIX

Jack agreed that it made sense to wait for Weston and estimated it would be at least an hour and a half before he arrived.

"The timing works for me," Jack reported. "It will give me time to finish up a few things before we go. And there should still be enough light left to look around when we get there. In the meantime you can take a break and relax. There's a nice restaurant down the block in case you're hungry, and I'll give you space in the office to unwind."

Olivia wasn't hungry and didn't want to unwind. She wanted to stay sharp, on top of everything going on.

"I wouldn't spend too much time outside, though," Jack continued. "The weather is hotter than usual right now and the bugs have been bad. You don't want to get mean bites all over."

"No, I don't," Olivia agreed. But I've already been bitten by this case, she thought. She was unable to put things on a back burner and take time to unwind. Instead, Olivia decided to use the waiting time to go on the computer and learn as much about Amanda as she could.

"If I could use one of the computers in the office that would be best," she replied.

Jack looked at Olivia intensely. "You want to check out everything about Amanda, right?"

"Naturally," Olivia replied.

"Obviously, you're convinced she's still alive," Jack added reluctantly. "That's a mistake."

"I'm certainly not convinced she's dead," Olivia answered. "I wouldn't be out here hunting if I was."

"Do as you please," Jack said as he led Olivia into a small room adjacent to his office, where he gave her a laptop computer to browse on.

Olivia took the computer gratefully and sat down on an old, wobbly couch in the corner. Then she quickly opened it up. This room was stuffier and warmer than the main office. It was harder to breathe here, made Olivia sleepy. After Jack left, Olivia played with the computer, and in just a few moments, Amanda's Facebook page popped up.

31

The page was surprisingly lively and upbeat, filled with photos of Amanda and Tye. They were surrounded by friends, happy and smiling. Olivia looked at her carefully. Amanda was certainly beautiful with her long, auburn hair, a dazzling smile, and light, carefree manner. Tye, standing beside her, seemed much more formal and buttoned up. Despite their differences, they seemed to be a good couple, well connected to one another. A wide variety of friends surrounded them, and there were assorted photos of them playing tennis with friends, walking in the woods, lounging on beaches, and listening to concerts under the trees. It looked like Amanda had been leading a happy life. The notes she'd written and messages received showed nothing out of order either. There was nothing here that was foolhardy and would suggest that Amanda had a craving for danger, or needed to place herself in harm's way.

Olivia then flipped to Tye's page, which was more orderly. It was filled with a few of his friends and family and photos of the homes he designed in various stages of being built. Olivia also saw an older couple on the page, who she assumed were his parents.

A huge wave of sadness suddenly gripped Olivia as she shut the computer down. There was only so much social media could tell her. Who could ever know what was lurking within when they simply looked at the outer forms of a person's life? Who could know what strange destiny was waiting just a few steps away? Was there ever a way to stop or change the trajectory of fate?

Olivia began to think of Todd and the harrowing death he'd experienced down in Key West. But Todd was murdered, and it seemed unlikely that had been Amanda's fate. The most likely and worst possibility was that she had come upon gators or crocs, been assaulted by them. Olivia knew that most people on the case felt that was what happened. Still, Olivia couldn't shake the feeling that something else had taken place. There was no reason for her to feel that way, she just did.

Olivia thought of Wayne for a second and what he would say about it all. She valued his insight and planned to call him later when she returned to her hotel. Then she closed her eyes and without realizing it, succumbed to the thick heat in the room, falling into a light sleep.

Olivia dreamt the sun was going down on the swamp as fierce birds called wildly to each other. The sounds of their cries were agitating, almost a harbinger of danger ahead. In her dream Olivia looked fervently around below for some signs of human life. To her sorrow there wasn't any. Only gigantic, primal reptiles starting to move closer to one another.

Olivia opened her eyes with a shock then to see both Jack and Weston standing in front of her. More time had elapsed than she realized. She was relieved to be awakened from the dream and still disturbed by it.

"My goodness." Olivia jumped up, surprised and embarrassed.

"It's fine, it's good," Jack replied, "nothing wrong with a little nap before we take off into the swamps."

*

Olivia, Jack, and Weston piled into the open water boat that was going right to the spot where Amanda had disappeared. It was a similar boat to the one Amanda had been in, and Olivia realized they were going to arrive at roughly the same time. There would be still enough light to see, but twilight would be coming quickly with a haze falling everywhere. Weston stood beside Olivia, tall and straight, much more somber than Olivia had remembered him being. This was obviously not something he was pleased about. He hadn't expected to be here now, but neither had she.

"Look over there, dragnets are being formed along the banks to find Amanda," Weston said, leaning over the edge of the boat. He pointed to groups of people gathering along the far shores. "It's dangerous to search here. They're taking their lives in their hands."

Olivia moved slightly away from him and looked at clusters of volunteers gathering in the twilight to aid in the search. They all had to believe Amanda was alive, too, thought Olivia. Or else, what would bring them out like this?

"I don't know how you could have even thought of coming on this trip alone," Weston said as the boat slowly pulled out into the muddy waters. "Not only do people need incredible guides here, but the insects alone are vicious." Weston slapped his wrist as he spoke, killing a small bug.

Olivia understood his concern and was even glad he was there. "Thanks for coming," she said.

As the boat rolled through sluggish swamp waters and high grass, the three of them grew silent, taking in both the surroundings and the awful reality of Amanda's disappearance.

"I have no idea how her husband is holding up," Weston said suddenly, surprising Olivia.

"Tye's a strong guy," Jack answered fitfully as more little bugs flew into the boat. Olivia wondered how Jack knew Tye was strong, but said nothing.

"Tye's good at keeping up a front at least," Weston answered.

33

Jack turned a moment and looked at him. "What else can he do? Will it bring his wife back if he crumbles and falls?"

"Nothing will," Weston murmured under his breath. "Once someone is gone, it's over."

Olivia took a deep breath. "You're being pessimistic," she said.

"Realistic," Weston instantly countered.

"Why are we here if it isn't possible to bring her back?" Olivia retorted.

Jack and Weston smiled at each other.

"We have to go through the paces," Weston finally replied in a low tone. "The law requires it."

"We have to look like we're searching, but not search really?" Olivia was offended.

"I didn't say that," Weston replied, staring out at the darkening sky. "We can search all we want, so can everybody, but what will we find at this point? Be realistic!"

Olivia wondered what Weston had been through in his life to feel hopeless.

"Maybe the most realistic thing is expect a miracle." Olivia was determined to counter the heavy mood he was creating around them. She wasn't just going through the paces for show, or to fulfill an official requirement. Olivia was determined to find out where Amanda was now and what actually had happened to her.

Weston scoffed and was about to reply when the boat shook and made a sudden halt.

"This is it, this is the stop the tour took a break at. Take a look around," Jack announced.

As far as Olivia could see, they were squarely planted in the middle of nowhere. Weston walked to the edge of the boat and leaned over.

"My God," he exclaimed, "no-man's-land."

Jack came over. "No, it's alligator land, snakes land, this is their habitat. And there's a hiking trail right there, carefully carved around the swamp. It goes on for a while, leads to the back of the swamp and beyond."

"It leads to the huts in the back?" asked Olivia.

"Yes, that's right," said Jack.

Weston was fascinated by the trail. "You mean Amanda got off the boat and walked out onto that?"

"She did," answered Jack glumly. "You can't blame us that she did something so crazy."

"Crazy is right," Weston flung back.

"She was obviously looking for something important to her," Olivia murmured, staring at the strange hiking trail.

"A Nile croc," Jack answered in a scathing tone.

"I don't believe that for a minute," Olivia replied.

"That's what she told us," Jack retorted.

"Olivia's right," Weston chimed in. "No one in their right mind would go off on a trail like this, looking for a croc. And there's no evidence that she was crazy."

"Her action is evidence enough, isn't it?" Jack said strongly.

Weston shook his head. "I agree with Olivia on this point," he said. "There's something else Amanda had to be after."

Jack stared at both of them. "Whatever Amanda really wanted is your business, not mine," he said, irritated. "I just take people for tours and ninety-nine point nine percent of the time, bring them back safe and sound. And happy."

"Okay." Olivia had enough of the banter. "Do you have boots for me and Weston to put on?"

"Why?" Jack became fitful. "You now plan to go out and walk that trail like Amanda?"

"We have to," said Olivia. "There's no choice about it. If she left something behind chances are that's where we'll find it."

"What do you expect to find? Everything's washed away by now." Jack was incredulous.

"So, I'll see what she saw, I'll feel what she felt." Olivia wasn't budging.

"Go get the boots," Weston said to Jack bluntly. "I'll go sloshing along with Olivia for a little while."

Without another word Jack went to the back of the boat to get big, heavy rubber boots for them to wear.

*

Once they were out of the boat, the boots hugged the shifting ground Olivia and Weston walked on. She was glad to have Weston beside her as they slowly trudged along. The squishy sound of boots in water, bird cries above, and the plop of animals falling into the water and up on the stones accompanied them as they moved along.

They had to walk carefully, as all kinds of animals slithered along. Amanda had done this alone, Olivia thought. Where was she going? What did she want? Maybe just to break free of other passengers on the tour for a few minutes? Olivia could relate to that; she wanted to break free of Weston herself right now. Had Amanda wanted to stand alone amidst untouched nature? There was something ennobling and powerful about walking a trail like this alone. Had Amanda felt stifled or controlled in her relationship with Tye? Maybe Amanda craved freedom and nature, without any holds. It seemed that way to Olivia as she stood there in Amanda's footsteps.

"Only a few steps more. We're not going far." Weston held tightly onto Olivia's elbow.

"We'll be fine," Olivia countered, wishing that she was out here alone. Weston was oppressive.

"Nothing's fine out here," Weston replied as Olivia looked through the high grass and in between the shadows that were forming.

"Everything is fine," she responded. "Everything is exactly as it should be." Olivia was moved by the life around her, living together in harmony.

"Okay, enough." Weston was irritated. "A few more minutes and we'll return."

"I first want to go to the hut up ahead," Olivia objected. In the far shadows Olivia could make out the shape of a small hut. It was close enough on the trail. Had Amanda gone into it and gotten caught? "I want to look inside it."

"Wait a minute. There's no reason for it." Weston was adamant. "That hut's deserted, probably filled with spiders and bugs of all kinds."

"Let's get closer and see," said Olivia. "We're only a few feet away."

Weston suddenly put both hands on Olivia's shoulders to stop her.

Olivia shook him off. "We're almost there," she repeated. "A few more steps." Then she ran up ahead as fast as she could through the mud and high grass.

Weston came up behind her quickly and they both arrived at the hut at the same moment.

"See, it's deserted!" he yelled.

"Maybe not!" Olivia yelled back as she leaned forcefully against the fragile, moldy wooden door.

"Stop!" Weston demanded. "The place has got to be filled with cobwebs, beetles—"

Olivia thrust her body against the door and pushed as hard as she could, until part of it fell to the side.

Amazed, Weston grabbed her hand as they stared inside.

"Empty," Olivia breathed, as she looked around carefully.

"I told you, no one's been here in ages," Weston echoed.

Suddenly Olivia spotted a long, slithering snake gliding toward them at top speed.

"A snake," she called out as it started hissing.

Weston thrust Olivia quickly to the side, pulled a large piece of wood from the splintered door and placing it in front of them as a shield.

"We've invaded his home! Let's get out of here!" Weston demanded. He grabbed Olivia and pushed her back onto the wet hiking trail to the waiting boat.

"What are the chances Amanda's alive? None." Weston breathed hard. "If the alligators didn't get her, the snakes did. I told you, there's nothing left to find."

CHAPTER SEVEN

Upon returning to her hotel in Key Largo, Olivia immediately called Wayne and told him what was going on.

"Talk to Frank next," Wayne said without a moment's hesitation. "The news is out that he was the guide on Amanda's tour. He was the last to see her alive."

"Haven't the police spoken to Frank already?" asked Olivia.

"They probably have," Wayne responded. "But it's not the same. He's got to have seen something that no one is aware of. Help him remember it. Let him tell you something he wouldn't otherwise say. Go, give it a try. And do it fast. This case could go cold in no time."

Olivia shook her head hard. "But we've just started."

"I know," said Wayne. "But time is of the essence, especially in the glades. Every day that passes the chances of finding Amanda alive go dramatically down."

Olivia knew it was so.

"Are you okay down there?" Wayne suddenly sounded concerned. "They're taking good care of you?"

"Yes, the cops are watching over me," Olivia replied. "They sent Weston to join me on the tour of the swamp."

"Who's Weston?" asked Wayne.

"He's a cop on the force. Weston's smart and careful, but he has no hope of finding Amanda alive," Olivia replied downheartedly.

"It's hard to keep up hope in conditions like these," Wayne replied. "Lots of police give up early on. They've seen too much bad stuff. But it's true, someone like that can be a downer. I'm glad you're keeping in touch with me, though."

"I'm grateful for your input," Olivia responded.

"The most important thing is to keep your spirits up," Wayne continued.

"Don't I know it," said Olivia.

"Our dinner date's still on, isn't it?" Wayne quipped lightly then, changing the tone of the conversation, causing Olivia to smile.

"Absolutely," she said, "the first chance we get. Dinner in Key West near the water."

"Great," said Wayne, "I'm looking forward to it."

"Me too," Olivia responded.

"Please keep in touch," Wayne repeated. "Let me know how it's going. These are murky waters you're swimming in."

"I will for sure," Olivia replied, hanging up the phone, encouraged. Talking to Wayne gave her just the boost she needed. She felt ready now to get in touch with Frank and see what he had to add to the picture.

*

Jack gave Olivia Frank's phone number grudgingly. When she called, Frank reluctantly agreed to meet her downtown early the next morning.

"Do I have a choice about it?" he asked Olivia.

"It's important," Olivia urged him. "Amanda's life is at stake."

"Okay, I'll come," Frank relented. "I'll be waiting at the Blue Marlin, a fishing shack near an inlet at eight a.m. It's where the diving boats take off. Don't be late."

Olivia wondered why it was so important to be prompt, but didn't dare ask. Frank sounded skittish enough as it was and she didn't want to push him further. So, the next morning, she put on a paisley summer dress, smeared on lipstick, and took a cab to the Blue Marlin. Olivia wondered if Frank lived or worked in that part of town. She'd find out soon enough, though.

As the cab drove through the open streets, Olivia realized how much calmer and more relaxing Key Largo was than Key West. There wasn't that flow of Key West activity that constantly kept you swept you up in a whirl at all times of day.

Olivia leaned back against the cab and thought about Amanda and Tye for a moment. She needed to stay in touch with Tye as well. The police were keeping him informed of developments, but Olivia also wanted to know him better. As time went on Olivia's questions about Amanda were growing. Tye might well hold the key to the answers. Olivia still couldn't get her mind around how it was possible that Amanda got off the tour and went on a hike like that alone. On the surface it seemed she was asking for trouble. Only on the surface, though. And that was not good enough for Olivia.

The cab arrived in front of the Blue Marlin in no time. It was a small shack which sold sandwiches, coffee, and some last-minute equipment for divers. Olivia got out and walked in, hoping that Frank would spot her. In the photo Jack showed her of him, Frank was young, slim, and agile with dark, messy hair and very big eyes. Jack had said that Frank was basically shy about personal matters and Olivia should tread lightly. That was good advice, thought Olivia, excited to meet Frank.

Olivia stood inside for only a moment before a young man who looked like Frank's photo rushed up to her. He wore ripped jeans and an old shirt and had tattoos on his forearm.

"Frank?" Olivia asked.

"Yeah, Jack described you to me perfectly." He scrutinized her carefully. "You're pretty young to be doing crazy work like this, aren't you?"

"Thanks for coming to meet me," Olivia replied.

"What choice did I have?" Frank was defiant.

"I'm sorry to put you out." Olivia decided to tread very lightly with him.

"Okay, okay." Frank wasn't going for it. "Let's just sit down and get this over with." He walked in front of Olivia then to two stools at a counter at the edge of the restaurant. Olivia followed behind him with trepidation.

"What do you want from me?" Frank then asked when both of them had been seated and billows of a light breeze thankfully blew in from the water.

"I need to know more about the tour you took Amanda out on," Olivia started.

"You're blaming me for what happened?" Frank's head shot up swiftly.

"Nobody's blaming you for anything." Olivia was taken back by his response.

"They'll never find her. She's done," Frank continued. "Nobody survives something like this. And everyone knows that!"

For a second his words brought Olivia to a standstill. Along with those trying to find Amanda a dragnet of hopelessness was forming everywhere. Olivia was determined not to get pulled into it.

"Tell me about Amanda, what did you notice?" Olivia plunged forward.

"Why should I tell you?" asked Frank. "What difference does it make?"

"Even if she's not alive, at the very least we need to find her body, don't we?" Olivia tried to soothe the rough waters she was in with Frank. "You might have noticed something about her that could help me locate her."

Frank scoffed. "What would I notice? I don't pay attention to the passengers when I lead the tours. I pay attention to the scenery.

All different kinds of people come on board. Who cares who they are? They all just come and go."

Olivia didn't understand why Frank was being so defensive. What exactly he was hiding?

"Did Amanda talk to anyone in particular on the tour?" Olivia asked then. "Did you happen to notice that?"

"Actually, I did," Frank said, surprising Olivia. "She talked to someone who had a big camera with him. A good-looking guy named Denton. He was a little older than her, and came down from the state of Washington."

"You know a lot about him." Olivia was surprised. This was something new, and she found it interesting, even if it didn't amount to anything.

"I just happened to overhear them talking," Frank replied. "We get people from all over. Lots of filmmakers come down to spot a location."

Olivia found that fascinating. "Do you think that's what Denton was doing?"

Frank shrugged and looked up at the ceiling. "I have no idea and I couldn't care less. The two of them seemed to enjoy talking, though."

"Did they know each other before they got on the boat?" It was all Olivia had and she had to pursue it.

"Listen, enough's enough! I have no idea and nobody does," exclaimed Frank. "And it doesn't matter anyway. People meet all the time and talk on the tours. Most come with someone, a few come alone. These two came alone, so they did some talking. Big deal. It's not my business, is it? And if I learned one thing in my life, it's to mind my own business."

Olivia smiled. Frank was shifty and restless, but smart in his own way.

"You haven't learned to mind your own business, though, have you?" Frank suddenly turned on Olivia. "One question after another. It's never enough, is it?"

Olivia quieted down and looked back at him. Something was definitely bothering him and Olivia needed to know what.

"You didn't know Amanda before the tour, did you?" Olivia asked bluntly then.

"No, I didn't." Frank shook his shoulders quickly, as if shaking off a bug. "Did I know her? Did I kill her? The questions never end." Frank's voice grew higher, ringing out into the hot day.

"I didn't ask if you killed her, just if you knew her," Olivia corrected him.

"Same thing, isn't it?" Frank shuddered. "You cops have all kinds of ways of playing with our heads. But I'm onto you."

"I'm not playing with anything, I just need a straight answer," Olivia retorted.

"Straight, crooked? What are you talking about?" Frank grew angry. "Are you saying now that I'm not answering right? I'm not giving you what you're after?"

"I'm not saying that at all." Olivia was put off. "I just asked if you knew Amanda."

"Yeah, and what else do you want to know? Did I steal her away from her husband and sleep with her down in the swamp? Next thing I know you'll haul me in for rape, like a lot of the poor idiots down here."

Olivia had no idea what he was talking about. Frank was off the charts and Olivia briefly wondered if he was on a drug of some kind.

"I wasn't thinking that," Olivia answered quickly. "How could anyone sleep with Amanda down in the swamp? She was in the boat the whole time, and you only took a rest stop for a few minutes."

"Exactly my point," Frank shot back. "I never left the boat, everyone saw me there. She said she'd be gone about ten minutes or so. We all waited for her a long time."

"Why did you let her go by herself?" Olivia had to know more.

"Why did I let her go?" Frank was indignant. "She was a big girl, wasn't she? What business was it of mine? I don't run a babysitting service. The passengers get to do what they want!"

"Did Denton advise her not to go?" Olivia was fascinated.

"How would I know that?" asked Frank. "What do you think, that I'm in charge of what people do and say? I'm not. I never was! And neither are you!"

"I never said I was, either," whispered Olivia.

"But you think you are, don't you?" Frank replied. "You think you're better and smarter than all of us down here."

"No, I don't," Olivia tried to reply, but to her horror, Frank swiftly got up from the stool and in the flash of a second fled the restaurant. He flew out onto the deck, down the stairs, across the sand, and, before she knew it, was gone from sight.

Stunned, Olivia sat still a moment and stared. What had frightened him so? Where was he headed now? Olivia immediately took out her phone and called the police station.

Thankfully, Mike picked right up.

42

"Frank just ran away in the middle of an interview," she breathed.

"The guide on Amanda's tour?" Mike sounded shaken.

"That's right. He's definitely hiding something, or something about this has scared him to death. You've got to find out more."

"We'll pick him up right away." Mike was all over it.

"Have you spoken to him yet?" Olivia was shaken as well.

"Yeah, we have, just briefly," Mike said. "But his running away like this is something else."

"Take him in for questioning right away," Olivia urged.

"Don't worry, we will," Mike replied.

CHAPTER EIGHT

Olivia finished her coffee and left the Blue Marlin to make her way to the police station. Key Largo was small enough that they should be able to find Frank and take him in no time. As she got into a taxi, her phone rang. Weston was on the other end, confirming it.

"Good work," Weston said the moment Olivia picked up. "We've got Frank in custody and are bringing him in right now. Come on down to the station and join us for the grilling."

Olivia was grateful to be included. "I'm on my way," she said "Thanks for letting me know."

"You're doing a terrific job, Olivia," Weston replied in a gruff tone. "And at least we're working on dry land now, not in that lousy swamp."

*

Olivia sat in the interrogation room with a few others waiting for the police to arrive with Frank. When they finally walked in Frank looked hot, sweaty, and frazzled. The minute he saw Olivia, he threw her a vicious glance.

"She's the reason I'm here, isn't she?" he burst out. "I knew no good would come from talking to her."

"Sit down and be quiet." A cop standing beside him pushed him down into the chair.

"I didn't do anything to anyone," Frank insisted. "You got no proof, you got nothing."

"This is just a regular interrogation," Mike quickly intervened.

"You got me once on a lousy case of shoplifting," Frank continued, "but that was it. It came to nothing. You let me go."

"That's not why you're here now," Mike stopped him.

"No, that's right. I'm here because of her!" Frank pointed at Olivia furiously.

"You're here because you were one of the last ones to see Amanda alive," Weston swiftly interrupted, as Tommy, another officer, entered the room.

Tommy walked straight up to Frank. He seemed to know him.

"I talked to you about this before," Frank said loudly. "I told you everything I know."

"Yes, you did," Tommy tried to reassure him. "Just answer the questions they've got for you now and you'll be fine."

"They're trying to lock me up." Frank's voice became shrill.

"No, they're not. They just have questions for you." Tommy spoke in a soothing tone.

"Okay," Frank sat up straighter and stared at the police. "Go ahead, ask me!"

Olivia watched in fascination. Frank was a loose wire, if ever she saw one. Of course it was possible that he was this anxious just because police were around. In and of itself, his volatility didn't mean he was guilty, Olivia reminded herself.

"Why'd you run away from Olivia in the middle of an interview?" Tommy started.

Frank didn't blink an eye. "Because I didn't like her. She irritated me. I was in my rights to get away."

"Did Amanda also irritate you?" Weston stood up and joined in.

Frank seemed surprised by the question. "Not at all. There's no comparison between them. Amanda was nice, she was pretty. Olivia's a shrew. She's mean as they come."

Olivia blanched, wondering what the police officers would think about her now. What in the world had she had done to make Frank feel that way? She had no idea.

"Why was Olivia mean? Because she kept asking you questions?" Weston got into it with him.

"That's right!" Frank replied. "She shot one question at me after another. Wouldn't cut it out."

"That's her job," Mike informed him. "Olivia's not here to win a popularity contest."

"Well, I didn't like it," Frank retorted. "Women like that get under my skin."

"Did Amanda also didn't get under your skin?" Mike spoke forcefully now.

"Not at all. Why should she?" Frank looked confused.

"You told Olivia that Amanda was talking to a nice-looking guy on the tour, Denton." Mike pursued it.

"So, Olivia told you everything I said?" Frank bared his teeth. "You're telling me she's also a snitch?"

"She's a terrific detective, that's what she is," Weston snapped at him.

45

"Of course she told us what you said. That's her job, isn't it?" Mike added.

"Yeah, so what?" Frank looked bewildered. "Let her talk to whoever the hell she wants to. Just not me."

"You're sure you weren't jealous of Amanda and Denton?" Mike continued.

Frank suddenly guffawed. "Me, jealous? Of what?"

"You got someone in your life for yourself, Frank?" Mike was turning up the heat.

"I sure do," Frank snapped, "I got all I want. The girls like me."

"But do you like them? That's the question, isn't it?" Mike snapped back.

"I like them just fine if they do what I want." Frank suddenly came to life.

"And if they don't?" Weston burst in.

Frank guffawed again. "That's my business."

Olivia was disturbed by the line of questioning, but found it interesting at the same time. They were trying to get at any underlying motive Frank could have had, for seeing to it that Amanda hadn't returned from the swamp.

"Tell us more about Amanda." Tommy stepped in then.

"There's nothing else to tell," Frank uttered. "I told you all I know already. She was a passenger on that lousy tour. She hung out with Denton. When it was time for a break, she wanted to go out alone on the trails."

"You've seen passengers do that before?" Tommy asked. "Do people get off the boat during the breaks?"

"As a matter of fact, no! I haven't seen it myself," Frank retorted. "But so what?"

The officers all suddenly looked at each other at the same moment. Every question brought them to a dead end. Where were they going with this, anyway?

But suddenly, Frank continued himself, unruffled, "After Amanda didn't come back, I put in a call into the cops right away. Where's the crime in that?"

"None at all that I can see," Tommy reassured him again. "So, why did you really run away from Olivia while you were talking? Tell us that and it will go better for you."

"You're sure?" asked Frank.

"Positive," said Tommy.

Frank cringed. "Listen, my little lady isn't happy catching me talking to other gals alone. That's who she is! And she can be a

46

tiger about it, if you know what I mean. She also happens to work right near the Blue Marlin. It suddenly hit me that for all I knew she was out for her morning stroll. The last thing I needed was to have her spot me sitting there, talking to Olivia. I'd have hell to pay then."

Tommy wrinkled his brow. "You're telling me now that you didn't want your girlfriend to find you and Olivia together alone? That's why you ran away?"

"Something like that." Frank seemed to feel better.

"But you told us a different story a minute ago. You said you ran away because you couldn't stand Olivia," Tommy went on.

Frank made a sour face. "That too," he replied. "Lots of things were working on me at the same time. I've had enough aggravation with this situation to last me. I don't need my girlfriend upset with me too."

"Okay. So, tell us what you think happened to Amanda. Just for the record," Mike broke in.

"How the hell do I know?" Frank repeated.

"What's your guess?"

"My guess is the gators got her." Frank's voice lowered. "Look, people come down to the glades at their own risk. Some like tormenting the animals, they think they're better than them. But you know what I've learned after all these years here? No one's smarter than the animals! In fact, the alligators and crocs are much smarter than us."

Olivia shivered, shaken by Frank's vehemence.

"Lots of people don't even see the danger down here." Frank was on a roll. "They think the gators and crocs are toys or playthings. If they go too far, these folks can find out different pretty fast. So, that's what I think happened."

"Anything else?" Tommy joined in now.

"No," said Frank. "Except maybe Amanda ran into one of the guys on the trail."

"Doubtful." Tommy shook his head.

"What guys?" asked Olivia, alert and distressed.

Frank turned to straight to Olivia. "There's loonies that sometimes drift around the swamp. Some of them are much worse than the gators. They're rotten sex addicts too." Frank seemed to be enjoying taunting her.

Stunned, Olivia looked at Weston for more information. Weston just shrugged and made light of it, though.

"Yes, of course, we get our fair share of perverts in these parts," he said, "but there's absolutely no reason to think one of

47

them was out there in the swamps. It doesn't make sense. They very, very rarely go there. Why would they? There's no reason to dwell on that idea at all. It's a detour if I ever saw one."

Frank waved his hand back and forth, taunting the police now. "Sure, don't tell anyone about those fellas, it's not good for business, is it? Or anything else, is it?"

Mike and Tommy grimaced then at the same moment.

"Okay, you listen to me, Frank," Mike said then. "I have nothing here to hold you, but I'm letting you know you're still part of this investigation anyway."

Frank bristled. "Why the hell am I? Because I was guide on her boat for a few hours?"

"Because we need any lead we can get. Go home and think about it carefully. Think hard! Remember whatever you can remember and bring it to us as soon as possible!" Mike added.

"I told you everything I know." Frank looked around the room, agitated, as if hunting for a way to get out. "Don't put your lousy problems on my shoulders. I got enough of my own. And whatever you do, don't sit around waiting for me to solve the mystery! That's up to you."

CHAPTER NINE

There was no way they could hold Frank and the cops let him go. "He's not guilty of anything but being a nervous wreck," Tommy was the first to comment.

"He's nervous for a reason, though, isn't he?" Mike joined in.

"Frank's always nervous," Tommy said. "What do we have on him though? Nothing."

"He lied to us," Weston commented. "First he said he ran away because of Olivia, then he changed his story to blaming his girlfriend."

"That's not a lie," Tommy objected. "He told only half the truth in the beginning. More came out later."

"Then he switched again and tried to blame it on a few of the pervs that drift around," Weston added. "He was obviously grasping at straws."

"He also told me to meet him at the Blue Marlin," Olivia chimed in. "If his girlfriend was close by and he didn't want her to see us, why did he choose that spot?"

A short moment of silence fell upon them all.

"Good point," Tommy had to agree. "Frank probably chose the Blue Marlin because he works close by. As I recall he helps on the diving boats. Most likely he couldn't take more time away right now."

Olivia still felt jarred by the entire encounter. "Frank's a loose wire if I ever saw one," she commented.

"He has no record of ever hurting anybody." Tommy seemed dead set on protecting him. But Olivia did feel better to hear that.

"It's good we brought him in," Mike seemed to be winding up the meeting. "What about this Denton guy, who Amanda was on the tour with? Anybody talk to him?"

"I spoke to him at length," Weston informed them. "He's a nice guy, smart and interesting. Frank was right, he's a filmmaker. Denton came down from Washington to scout locations for a film he's making on sudden death."

"Sudden death?" Olivia exclaimed.

"Really?" Mike also found that troubling. "Well, he got more than he bargained for, didn't he? He got a real life story."

"Yeah, and he seemed pretty shook up about it," Weston continued. "He kept saying he couldn't believe what happened. Amanda was such a fun person, so beautiful and alive."

"What else did he say?" Mike was all over it now.

"He said she was interesting to talk to and enjoying the tour thoroughly. She was upset when the boat stopped where it did and wasn't going any further. She was intrigued by what lay just a little ahead."

"I heard she was hoping to see a Nile croc," said Olivia.

"Yes, that's right," Weston continued. "Denton mentioned that. But he said that mostly Olivia kept repeating that she didn't want to miss even one thing that was out there waiting for her. She had no idea when she'd been back again."

"That was a premonition," Tommy murmured then. "People have them all the time before they die."

"I don't know about that," Weston replied. "Denton made a point of saying that she didn't seem to have any sense of danger up ahead. She felt completely at home in the swamp."

"Lots of tourists feel at home and don't sense danger," Mike commented.

"That's good," Tommy added. "Most of them are safe and sound."

"Except when they're not," Mike added, getting ready to go now.

Olivia stood up then, eager to leave and sort everything out slowly. Was she herself aware of the danger she was in? She felt oddly at home here also.

"Let's go for some coffee," Weston quickly suggested to Olivia as she began walking to the door.

Olivia stopped, surprised by the offer. "Sure," she agreed, "we can go for a little while." It was always good to talk and find out what Weston had on his mind.

*

Weston took Olivia to a small café around the corner, ordered some coffee, and they sat down outside under a shady tree.

"Quite a case, isn't it?" Weston started, probing for Olivia's response. He seemed genuinely interested in her feelings about it.

"It's hard," she replied. "I don't have a good enough take on Amanda yet. I plan to go back to speak more to her husband."

"That's a good idea." Weston nodded.

"And I can't help feeling I should go back to the swamp again, too," Olivia murmured.

Weston's face grew tight. "That's too much. There are plenty of groups searching every inch of the territory. Including trained dogs. They haven't found a thing either, not a shred of evidence."

"Could be all the more reason for me to go," said Olivia, feeling the swamp calling to her, and not sure why.

Weston looked at Olivia oddly. "You seem incredibly driven," he said, as their coffee arrived.

"I'm incredibly thorough," Olivia corrected him.

"I heard that your fiancé was murdered down here," Weston continued. "That had to be a terrible shock."

Olivia was startled by his comment. "Yes, of course, Todd's death was a terrible shock," she said. "But it was a while ago. I've dealt with it."

"These things can take time," Weston replied. "The aftereffects of shocks can hang on for a very long time."

Olivia suddenly felt uneasy. Was he implying that she was still in shock, that there was something wrong with her?

"Are you saying I'm doing this work because I'm in shock?" she asked, offended.

"No, not at all," Weston quickly corrected himself. "You're doing a great job. But it's also possible to be too driven. Then you can't let something go when you should, like wanting to return to the swamp! That can become an obsession. Obsessions drag you down, stop you from focusing where you should. A good cop needs to know what's important and what's not."

Olivia recognized what Weston was saying was true. But she didn't feel it applied to her. This wasn't the time to let go of searching in the swamp. Not by a long shot.

"What's wrong with obsessions?" Olivia took Weston on. "Absolutely nothing. They can even be good if they don't let you rest until you find the killer. Or find a person who's still alive."

"You're different from most women I've met," Weston said slowly. "You're smart, but also foolhardy."

Olivia didn't like that. She drank the rest of her coffee and decided to let him think what he wanted. There was no reason to get into an argument with him. She had no intention of sitting here defending herself.

"Tell me about every hut and structure within a few miles of those swamps." Olivia returned to the main issue, the search for Amanda.

Weston went along. "There's a hut about five miles down the trail. It's a bigger fishing shack that's mostly abandoned these days."

"Mostly?" Olivia raised her eyebrows.

"Yeah, fishermen used to be more active in these parts a while back," Weston recalled. "Then the shacks got used for other things. Photographers used them, painters, like that. As far as I know, no one occupies them at this time."

"Well, let's find out for sure." Olivia felt her tiredness vanish. "I want to go back to the shack and look for myself."

"Whoa." Weston held up his hand. "I'm not going back there again, and neither should you! There's no reason for it."

"There is a reason," Olivia objected.

"It's a very long shot," he insisted. "There are more important things to do first. It's really important for us to use our time wisely. Priorities are everything, especially in a case like this."

Olivia couldn't help but agree. "Thanks, Weston," she relented, thinking she'd go back to the swamp later on. There was no reason to discuss it with him further. She didn't need his stamp of approval. And he was trying to help, in his way. "Our talk has been useful," she added.

"Really?" Weston's face lit up. "I'm glad to hear that. It's very useful for us to have you on the case as well."

Olivia smiled. "I appreciate that."

"What's next now?" asked Weston.

"I'm not totally sure yet," Olivia replied. "I'll go back to my hotel in Key Largo now and take a few minutes to think it all over."

Weston looked at her oddly. "Okay, but let us know what you plan to do. It's tricky down here."

"I realize that," said Olivia.

"No," he continued. "I mean there are real potholes to fall into that you have no idea are just waiting for you."

"I'm sure there are," Olivia answered, a surge of emotion filling her now. "But I can't help feeling Amanda's still alive. I really do."

Weston stopped and stared at Olivia. "That's a wish," he uttered.

"It's more than a wish," she insisted.

"You have no rational reason to think that." Weston spoke somberly.

"What does reason have to do with it?" Olivia felt her eyes filling with tears of exasperation.

"Olivia, I'm sorry." Weston extended his hand and put it on hers. "I know this is rough. We all want to think Amanda survived, that's she alive somewhere waiting for us."

"Don't put her in the past tense," Olivia demanded.

"But we have to stay grounded in reality," Weston continued.

"Whose reality, exactly?" Olivia shot back. "My feeling could be just a wish, or it could be more than that!"

"Okay, call it a dream or a prayer then," Weston relented.

"Or it could be a sixth sense, telling me that Amanda's out there alive somewhere," Olivia responded.

Weston smiled slightly then, taking his hand away, as he and Olivia finished up their coffees and prepared to go their separate ways.

*

I'll find a way out of here if it's the last thing I do, Amanda barely whispered to herself, cramped together in the makeshift cabin. The heat was overpowering and her breath had grown ragged. He had been gone for a while now and didn't know that she'd already been able to rip her arms free of the heavy rope he'd bound her with. That was a huge step. After rubbing it against the back edge of the wheel, hour after hour, it had finally come loose. She was too weak now to make a break for the door though. He could be back at any moment and find her. He hadn't given her anything to eat or drink for many hours now, too. Sometimes he fed her and she rallied. Other times he sat there enjoying her begging for food.

"Help, help," Amanda suddenly called out again with what was left of her voice.

The sound of crickets and a faraway hooting bird answered.

I won't give up hope, she kept repeating to herself, over and over, like a mantra. My hope's all I have left. It will get me through. He won't get me. I won't allow it.

"Help," she howled once again through the small crack in the door, before she lifted her weary arms and wiped the sweat dripping from her forehead. Then, tremendously hungry and dizzy, she dropped her head back down on the pile of dead grass and fell into an uneasy sleep.

CHAPTER TEN

After leaving Weston, Olivia quickly went back to her hotel and decided to call Jack to arrange for another visit down the swamp. She'd find someone else to go with. To Olivia's disappointment, Jack wasn't picking up, so she left a message.

"Jack, this is Olivia, give me a call as soon as you can. I want to go back to look at the shack in the swamp five miles down from where Amanda disappeared. Thanks for everything."

Then she hung up and rested the sofa for a moment, going over everything that had happened. It had gotten dark outside suddenly with thick thunderclouds forming in the sky. Lying there, Olivia could hear the winds whirring. It felt like a thunderstorm was about to break. This was a good place to ride it out.

Olivia closed her eyes when to her surprise she suddenly heard rapid knocking on her door. Startled, she sprang to her feet.

"Who is it?" Olivia called out.

"It's me, Irma," a voice on the other side of the door answered.

Olivia went right to the door. "Irma who?" she asked without opening up.

"I'm Amanda's good friend," the voice continued. "I have pictures of me and her together. Don't be afraid. Please open the door."

With the latch on, Olivia slipped the door open a crack.

A young, slender woman stood outside, trembling. She looked at Olivia through the crack in the door and then held up large photos of her and Amanda.

"Please let me in for a minute. I have to talk," Irma pleaded.

Olivia opened the door immediately.

"Oh, thank you, thank you, I'm so grateful to see you." Irma's words spilled out one after another as thunder outside began rolling and rain splashed at the windows. "I've come down to the Keys with a few other good friends of Amanda. We're here to join the search teams," she continued.

"Sit down, Irma." Olivia wanted to calm her. "It's wonderful that you came to help. "Where's the rest of Amanda's family?"

"Amanda's an only child and her parents are in Europe for the summer. We actually haven't told them yet," Irma quickly continued. "Not until we have more news. Tye's parents are gone, vacationing as well."

"I see," said Olivia.

"This is a nightmare, a nightmare," Irma kept muttering. "Amanda and I are like sisters. We've been best friends since high school, talk almost every day."

"Thank you so much for coming to see me," Olivia replied.

"We've got to do everything we can to find her." Irma stared into Olivia's eyes.

"I'm doing my best," Olivia assured her. "We're in a rough situation."

"I know we are. But we've all heard great things about you," breathed Irma.

"Tell me more about Amanda, please," said Olivia. "Anything that could help me figure out where she could be."

Irma put her hands over her face then, as if about to sob.

"Try your best," Olivia tried to soothe her.

"I'm convinced something bad has happened to her," Irma said finally.

"You're worried the crocodiles or alligators got her?" Olivia asked.

"No." Irma stopped in her tracks. "Not really. It's true Amanda's a daredevil, but she's not a fool. She knows how to be safe whatever she does. She's gone on extreme adventures before and nothing's happened! Amanda's smart, she's careful."

"What do you think happened to her now?" Olivia shivered.

"I don't know but I can't stop thinking about it." Irma leaned closer to Olivia. "I've been turning everything over and over in my mind and decided I had to tell you something."

"Yes, please do," Olivia was completely gripped by the situation.

"Amanda and Tye have been going through a hard time," Irma said finally.

This was the first time Olivia had heard anything about this. The information hit her like a bolt of lightning.

"Olivia and Tye actually came down here for their anniversary," Irma continued. "They wanted to see if they could patch things up between them."

"Patch things up? Were things were so bad that they were thinking of splitting?" Olivia breathed.

"It was a definite possibility," Irma said tentatively as the winds outside blew harder.

"Tell me more, please," said Olivia.

"Their relationship was nothing at all like everyone imagined," Irma went on. "Tye's a rough customer. He's dominating! He does it all quietly, behind the scenes."

"How was Tye dominating her?" Olivia was aghast. Was Irma talking about domestic abuse?

"Tye wanted things his way when he wanted it!" Irma looked frightened to be speaking about this at all. "This is just between you and me, of course," she added.

"You can speak freely to me," Olivia answered. "Anything you say could help us find Amanda."

"Tye plays mind games with people. He has to be in control," Irma added quickly. "He couldn't control Amanda, though, and it was driving him nuts."

"Was he like that before they got married?" Olivia was appalled.

"A little, but it got much worse after the wedding," Irma continued. "At first Amanda didn't think much about it, but then it started to take a toll. Thank God she was able to talk to me about it. First he'd tell her she was beautiful, then in the next breath he'd say she was growing fat. And of course, she wasn't. Amanda was always beautiful."

That's awful," breathed Olivia.

"One minute he'd praise her, the next take her down," Irma continued. "It was very confusing. Amanda began doubting herself more and more. I saw it happen in front of my eyes. She became shakier and shakier. Soon she went back to the extreme sports she used to love. She started bungee jumping and dueling again."

"Because of Tye?" Olivia was mesmerized.

"It was Amanda's way of feeling strong and powerful. She once told me it made her feel more powerful than both danger and death. It was how she conquered the dark forces." Irma's voice grew low and choppy.

"What dark forces?" asked Olivia, appalled.

"I thought that stuff was all over," Irma continued, bypassing Olivia's question. "I thought once Amanda married and settled down, she'd feel safe and happy."

"She didn't though?" murmured Olivia.

"In the beginning yes, later on, no," Irma reported.

"Did she have to conquer dark forces before?" Olivia needed specifics.

Irma was now finding it harder to speak. "Amanda was alone a lot growing up, and felt unprotected. But she always had a wild streak. Doing extreme sports was her way to feel stronger than anything bad that could happen to her."

Olivia felt a strong wave of compassion for Amanda as she listened to her friend speak.

"Is there any chance she's still alive? Any at all?" Irma burst into tears now. "Did the dark forces finally get her?"

"I need to know what dark forces you're talking about," Olivia repeated forcefully. "Are you referring to her husband?"

"Not necessarily," said Irma. "There's got to be lots of dark forces down in the Everglades though. And plenty of dark forces inside Amanda."

Olivia was beside herself. "Was Amanda terrified or enraged? Are you suggesting she could have committed suicide out there in the swamps?"

"No." Irma shuddered. "That would mean that death got her! She said it never would!"

"But is it possible she killed herself?" Olivia felt chilled.

"Maybe," Irma went on tentatively, barely looking at Olivia now. "Amanda actually talked about it a few times. She said one day she might get back at Tye by walking into a swamp and never returning. Then he'd have to live with it his whole life long."

Olivia was completely horrified. "She actually said that?"

"Yes."

"Well, it sounds like that's exactly what she did! Especially if she said it."

"No, she didn't do it!" Irma was insistent. "She said it but she didn't mean it. Amanda loved being overly dramatic. I think she even said it to Tye as well. She just wanted to frighten him and stop him from acting like he did. It was an extreme statement, but that was Amanda. She loved pushing the edges. She never would have done it though. Please believe me! She loved life more than anyone I know."

"So what do you think happened? Is Amanda hiding out from Tye now, to make him squirm and worry?"

"It's possible, but I don't know for sure." Irma broke down sobbing. "I'm telling you all I can right now. I really am, believe me."

*

After Irma left Olivia sat alone, shaking. The rains and winds had gotten stronger and the lights in her room flickered on and off. Irma's story had opened up a whole new avenue of exploration.

Was it possible that Amanda had left the boat purposely, knew exactly what she was doing? Was everything she did all based on vengeance?

Olivia's phone rang suddenly and she picked right up.

"I can't stop thinking about your case." Wayne was on the other end. "I've heard that some of the search teams are disbanding. No one's getting anywhere."

"Wrong," Olivia whispered back fervently, thrilled to be speaking to Wayne. "Just the opposite is true now."

"The opposite?" Wayne was startled.

"A friend of Amanda's just came to my hotel room. She said Amanda and Tye were having trouble in their marriage. She'd actually threatened him that she was going to walk into the swamps one day and not return."

"When did you hear that?" Wayne sounded amazed.

"Just now," Olivia gasped.

"You think she did this to get back at her husband?" Wayne shot back.

"A definite possibility," said Olivia.

"This could be the crux of it, then!" Wayne's voice rose. "Incredible that you got that information. If it's suicide it explains lots of things, doesn't it?"

"Except that we don't have a body," Olivia responded. "No one's found a thing. Nothing."

"Use your imagination," said Wayne then.

Olivia shook her head. "No, I don't buy that."

"What do you think?" Wayne sounded like he was on the edge of his seat.

"My gut tells me she's still alive somewhere," Olivia insisted.

"Is she grandstanding? Is she playing a game to get attention and drive her husband nuts?" asked Wayne.

"I wouldn't go that far, I just feel she's still around somewhere," said Olivia.

"I respect your feelings," Wayne answered, giving Olivia a bolt of strength.

"Thanks so much, Wayne," she replied. "Weston doesn't."

"Weston?" asked Wayne.

"He's that cop on the force who's a downer. Weston's convinced Amanda's dead, that I'm not facing reality."

Wayne paused. "You've got to be true to your own reality, Olivia," he said. "That's your job. Check out what you feel thoroughly, back up what you think."

Olivia smiled. "How'd you get to be so wise, Wayne?" she asked, grateful.

"It took a long time," he answered lightly. "But that's what good cops do! They don't follow standard roadmaps, they look into corners and side roads that no one realized were there. That's how cases get solved."

"This one, too?" Olivia asked. "Is it solvable, Wayne?"

"Especially this one. Every case is solvable." His voice got lower as a loud clap of thunder crashed and shook the room. "It's great that you got this information," Wayne continued. "Now, start with the obvious. It's often the wife or husband. Go look deeper into Tye."

"I plan to," agreed Olivia. "Just what I was thinking, too."

*

Olivia felt much better after speaking to Wayne, and decided to wait until the storm passed to see Tye. In fact, she decided to ask Tye to go to dinner, so they'd have plenty of time for him to tell all.

In the meantime, Olivia whipped out her laptop to go over Tye's social media thoroughly. She began feverishly scrolling through his pages. One after another they came up clean. He was successful, had good friends, and was engaged in all of the right activities. Everything he said about and to Amanda online expressed only love and admiration. There was nothing at all to reflect trouble in their relationship. Or to view him as dominating.

For a startling moment Olivia wondered if Irma had made all of this up. Did she have an ulterior motive? Was she creating a camouflage in order to cover up something entirely different? It seemed odd that nobody had heard anything at all of trouble in Amanda's marriage. And no one online had made any mention of Amanda being a daredevil, or craving extreme sports.

Olivia decided to take a break for a little while. She lay down on the couch, closed her eyes, and fell into a light nap as time passed gently.

The sound of her phone buzzing awakened Olivia suddenly. When she opened her eyes it was later than she realized. Dark out already. Olivia reached out for the phone and saw a text message flashing.

BREAKING NEWS: *Human remains found in alligator's mouth in swamp where Amanda went missing!*

59

CHAPTER ELEVEN

Olivia grabbed her phone and stared at it. Then she read the message over and over until it sank in. Human remains had been found in the swamp right near where Amanda had gone missing. And in an alligator's mouth! How was it possible after all this time? Had the alligator recently found her dead body? Olivia only prayed that Amanda hadn't been eaten alive.

Beside herself, Olivia grabbed the phone and called the station. Weston picked up immediately.

"Sorry to have told you this way!" he breathed. "I had no other choice. So many people have to be notified."

"It's true?" asked Olivia

"Yes, I'm sorry," he said. "Come meet us at the station. We're all going down to the spot where the remains were found."

Olivia shivered. "What's going on there now?"

"The remains are being collected," said Weston. "Do you want me to come to your hotel and pick you up?"

"That would be good," said Olivia, too shocked to do anything else. "I'll be downstairs in the lobby."

*

When Olivia and the police arrived at the swamp the area was cordoned off for only a special few to enter. Despite that, reporters and photographers had gathered on the outskirts, along with volunteers of all kinds, peering in. But despite the sizable crowd that had gathered, an eerie silence hung over the place. A sliver of the moon shone through the mist, shedding an eerie light in the heavy night air where a feeling of horror had taken hold.

Olivia walked into the cordoned off area with the police officers, grateful to be able to get up close. A strange dank odor filled the space. Thankfully, it was dark and she couldn't really make out the dead alligator sprawled a few feet away on the ground. Officials close up to the alligator were taking both the human remains and any other evidence they could find. Olivia watched Weston and Mike go right over and confer with one of them. Then Olivia looked out over the faces of people on the outside gazing in.

Everyone seemed desperate for any piece of information they could get.

Olivia walked over to Weston. "Is it her? Are they sure?" she asked in a low tone.

Weston looked shaken. "It's hard to tell because the body is so mangled," he replied. "They're gathering the remains carefully."

Olivia shuddered and walked away. This was not the outcome she'd expected or believed would take place.

Weston came up close behind Olivia then. "Mike is certain it's her," he went on. "It all fits the picture. Nobody can imagine who else it could be."

"Have you notified Tye?" asked Olivia quickly.

"Not yet," said Weston. "We need more information first. Mike wants to be absolutely positive."

"What's the next step?" asked Olivia, thinking Tye should have been the first one they called.

"What's left of the body will be taken right to the coroner," Weston continued. Once it's carefully examined, we'll have a better idea."

"You should call Tye and tell him yourself now," Olivia objected. "For all we know he could hear it on the news!"

"That's what I told Mike," Weston agreed. "Mike wants to tell Tye in person himself, but he said it's up to me."

The rippling sound of the crowd murmuring grew louder as Olivia and Weston spoke. She looked over toward them and suddenly saw two of the officers who had been collecting evidence carry something away in a large bag.

"Call Tye now," Olivia urged. "They're taking the evidence out."

Weston nodded and moved under a large tree, took out his phone, and dialed. After a long moment, he began to talk.

"Tye, this is Officer Weston Garland." He paused a moment.

"Put him on speakerphone, please," Olivia whispered.

Weston nodded, complied, and continued. "There's news I have for you," Weston went on. "Nothing definite has been confirmed as yet, but there is a significant development in the case."

"What?" asked Tye, his voice sounding raspy, as if he'd just awakened from sleep.

"Human remains have been found in an alligator's mouth down in the swamp right near where Amanda disappeared." Weston was trying to sound as official as possible.

"What?" Weston sounded truly alarmed. "What are you telling me?"

"Be calm please," Weston continued.

"Calm? Are you kidding? Human remains?" Tye was totally beside himself now.

"They're being taken to the coroner right now as we speak," Weston went on.

"Human remains? The coroner?" Tye couldn't seem to put it together, but suddenly broke into wracking sobs. "What are you telling me? What? I want to see Amanda immediately. Bring her here to me as soon as possible!"

Weston looked at Olivia, distraught. "We'll all be meeting at the coroner's in Key Largo, in about an hour," he said.

"I want to be there too," Tye wailed.

"Of course he must come," Olivia insisted, "he can't be left with this news alone."

"Yes, certainly, please join us," Wayne said to Tye back on the phone. "Be there in an hour. That'll give us all time to return."

As Olivia and Weston turned and walked close to the edge of the enclosure, one reporter heatedly waved Olivia over.

"Is it her? Are they sure?" the reporter asked fervently.

"We don't know, can't be certain yet," Olivia replied.

*

A small group gathered at the coroner's office, which was located in a long, low, steel-gray building at the edge of Key Largo. Mike and Weston went right inside the coroner's room to speak with him for a few moments. Olivia preferred to wait in the lobby. When she entered she saw Irma and Amanda's other friends, huddled together in the corner. Irma barely noticed Olivia come in and made no attempt to say hello. Olivia sat down there alone, drenched in the horror of what she'd just witnessed.

In a few moments Weston came out of the coroner's office and over to Olivia. Then Tye came running into the building, in total disarray. The minute Tye spotted Weston, he came over and grabbed him by the shoulders.

"Is it her? Are they sure?" Tye was breathing heavily.

"No, we're not sure of anything yet." Weston tried to calm him down.

"What do you mean?" Tye stopped and stared at him sharply.

"We've just talked to the coroner and he needs time," Weston continued.

"Time for what?" Tye seemed completely dazed.

"He needs time to carefully identify the body," said Weston. "It's so mangled, at first glance it's hard to say if we'll ever know, for sure."

"That's ridiculous. It's crazy," Tye was totally beside himself now. He put his head in his hands then and began sobbing. "You can't tell me this, I can't bear it."

Olivia looked at his deep distress and wondered again if what Irma had said was true. None of it computed, especially not now.

"What happens now?" Tye looked around wildly. "I demand that you let me see my wife's remains."

"There's nothing to see," Weston said slowly. "The best thing for now is to let us take you back to your hotel. Are you there by yourself?"

"Two friends are on their way down," Tye uttered. "The news is spreading."

"Maybe the best thing is for me to go get some coffee with Tye," Olivia interrupted. "I can keep him company until his friends arrive."

Tye agreed. "That's a good idea, very," he said.

"Okay, so let's get out of here then, and go back to the coffee shop in your hotel," Olivia suggested. "That's the best we can do for now."

The two of them turned to leave and Olivia suddenly saw Irma lurch away from the group and give Olivia and Tye a withering glance.

*

"I can't sit in the coffee shop now," said Tye fitfully as he and Olivia approached the hotel. "Come up to my room with me."

"Of course," said Olivia. "I'll order coffee up there."

They quickly got out of their cab and went right to his room. As soon as he entered, Tye fell down on the sofa and his phone started ringing relentlessly.

"I can't answer these calls," he muttered, "not now."

"You don't have to," Olivia agreed as she went over to the hotel phone and called up for hot coffee. "Anything else you want beside coffee?" she asked.

"I want Amanda home right away!" Tye suddenly wailed.

Olivia sat in the chair across from Tye as they waited for the coffee.

"It's not definite yet, nothing's definite, is it?" Tye murmured in a low voice.

63

"You're right," said Olivia. "Nothing's certain at all."

At that Tye looked up at Olivia, startled. "What are you saying exactly?"

"That nothing's definite yet," Olivia repeated, for the sake of both of them.

Tye sat up swiftly on the sofa at that thought. "But what are the chances the remains could belong to someone else?" he muttered.

"Very slim," Olivia agreed, "but there are still chances."

To Olivia's distress that thought did not seem to make Tye happy.

"Very slim chances, though," he murmured once again.

"You don't seem happy to hear that." Olivia felt uneasy.

"I'm not one for wild goose chases," Tye shot back strongly. "I'm not one to get my hopes up, just to be disappointed again and again."

That made perfect sense to Olivia, but still left her feeling peculiar. "What was your marriage really like, Tye?" she asked then in a hushed voice. "Were you disappointed by it again and again?"

"Not at all." His eyes opened wide and sparks flew. "I already told you that we were happy. I loved Amanda and she loved me."

"That's it? That wraps it all up?" Olivia needed this opportunity to find out what else went on.

A sudden knock on the door interrupted them. It was the coffee being brought to the room.

"Let them knock, don't answer," Tye exclaimed.

"It's the coffee," said Olivia.

"Let them leave it outside. I don't want anyone in here now," he insisted.

Olivia got up and went to the door. "Please leave it outside the door," she called. "Thanks."

Then she went back and sat down opposite Tye.

"I can't bear seeing anyone now," Tye explained. "Just people I know and am close to."

"Your friends will be here soon?" Olivia asked.

"Soon enough," he said, agitated.

Olivia felt mildly relieved. She had no idea who these friends were, but didn't want Tye to be going through this by himself.

"You asked me if I was disappointed in Amanda?" Tye went back to Olivia's line of questioning on his own.

Olivia was surprised. "Were you?" she asked again.

Tye seemed relieved to be talking about it. "Listen, in all marriages there are moments of disappointment. Sure, here and there, I was disappointed maybe, and so was Amanda. But overall

64

we were incredibly good together. We were happy. This was our anniversary celebration." The muscles under his eye started to twitch. "We were both determined to have a wonderful time."

This was similar to the story Tye had told them before. There was nothing wrong in his marriage. They were here to celebrate and that was that.

"Did you like Amanda's friends, as well?" Olivia couldn't help but ask.

"What difference does that make?" Tye suddenly seemed offended.

"You don't only marry a person," Olivia couldn't help add, "you also marry their friends and family. Is that what disappointed you?"

"You're smart, you're sharp." Tye jumped off the couch and started walking back and forth. "You're right, too. Amanda's friends could get under my skin. Especially Irma, who called Amanda every day. Irma couldn't get over that Amanda was actually married. She couldn't let go of the friendship they once had."

"Why should she let it go?" Olivia was puzzled.

"Why?" Tye looked disturbed. "Because I was Amanda's main person now. Irma was an old friend, and that was that. There was no reason for them to talk every day. Irma was jealous of our relationship, wanted to get in between."

"Are you sure of that?" asked Olivia.

"Positive." Tye stopped walking. "It was obvious to everyone. I even told Amanda a few times that Irma didn't mean her any good."

"Did Amanda agree?" asked Olivia, startled.

"No, she didn't, actually. She thought I was the one being jealous. I wasn't jealous, though, just irritated. Amanda didn't need another confidant. She had me at her side now for everything."

Olivia nodded slowly, taking the entire picture in. Irma considered Tye dominating because he'd wanted to be the most important person in Amanda's life now. The pieces of the puzzle were coming together, but did it really make any difference at this point? Remains had been found. Was the story over? Cased closed?

"I'll go bring the coffee in from outside the door," Olivia said then.

"Good idea," said Tye, "I could use a few strong cups. Then you can leave me here. I'll be fine alone. I need the time and my friends will be here in an hour."

*

65

This isn't going to go on forever, it can't, thought Amanda. There's a way out and I know it. And he's too stupid to keep me trapped forever like this. He's too frightened of something that just happened, too. Amanda didn't know for sure what it was, but he'd been different the last time he'd come back. He'd even brought her a plate of old food. Old food was good, it was enough for anyone. Amanda had grabbed the wilted peppers and pickles and eaten the rice with her bare fingers. He'd laughed when she'd done that.

"Pretty hungry, huh?" he'd sneered.

"Bring me food every time you come," she'd ordered. The crying and pleading hadn't worked. Amanda was now trying another track.

He'd laughed.

"Or you'll never know what hit you," she added. It was now her turn to frighten him. It had worked too, or partially at least.

"What the hell are you talking about?" He'd had a moment of fear.

"You know what I mean," she shot back.

"No I don't." The moment passed quickly. "But you do what I say or I'll throw you the hell into that river like a piece of old meat. You do just what I say! You hear me?" he yelled in his guttural voice.

"I hear you," Amanda snapped. Who was he anyway? He'd kept his mask on the entire time. Was he fronting for someone? Just doing his job? Sometimes it felt like that. Other times it felt personal, like he was settling old scores.

"What's in this for you?" Amanda once asked him.

Taken aback, he'd lurched to the side then. "You just keep your mouth shut, honey," he answered, or you'll never talk another day in your life."

CHAPTER TWELVE

Olivia returned to her hotel exhausted. She closed the door carefully and knew she had to unwind before trying to get to sleep. Too much had happened all at once and her mind was racing ceaselessly. Weston had promised to contact her the minute he had more news from the coroner. He'd also checked up on her while she was with Tye. Olivia had realized that Weston was unnerved by this too, and she was also bringing him strength and comfort. Of course he would never admit it. It was not his way. Even though Weston was definitely upsetting at times, Olivia liked him. She wondered who he really was, what he was hiding under the surface.

Olivia decided to take a long, warm bath to ease her nerves and relax. As she walked to the bathroom, she suddenly passed her front door, looked down, and noticed an envelope lying on the floor. It looked as if it had been slipped in under the door by someone.

Olivia went right to the envelope and opened it quickly. Inside was a handwritten note, words sprawled across the page.

You're on the wrong track, Olivia, it read. ***Check out Jack Healey's past. Look into Lorna Dempsey.*** There was no signature. Just those few lines.

Olivia's heart started pounding. Who had sent this? The note had to be referring to Jack Healey, the owner of the tour company. And who was Lorna Dempsey? Olivia's hand shook as she held the peculiar message.

Immediately, Olivia rushed to her computer and started looking more deeply into Jack's past. As she put his name into the search engine, she quickly discovered archived articles about his fantastic life. Olivia read one piece after another. As Jack had mentioned, he was a fifth-century tour guide in the Everglades. He'd joined in many battles over the glades to save them as a wildlife preserve. There was no way he was going to allow the glades to become another populated tourist trap. Jack had fought hard and was greatly respected. He'd also lobbied for the rights of the natives down here. Jack was married with a large family. Olivia remembered seeing their pictures hanging on his office wall.

Next, Olivia typed in the name Lorna Dempsey. Immediately a picture of a lovely young woman popped up. She'd gotten lost in the swamps, much as Amanda had, twenty years ago. Lorna was on one of Jack's tours as well and he'd been the guide. She hadn't gotten off the boat, though. It seemed a storm had blown up unexpectedly, rocking the boat and blowing her off, down into the waters below. There was a fuss about it for a while and a brief investigation. But most finally assumed it was a terrible accident and Lorna had simply drowned.

Questions had swirled around Jack and what exactly had gone on. Most of the questions had never been fully answered and although Jack had been brought in for questioning, he was quickly let go. Never charged with anything at all. The story subsided on its own. Whoever had written this note hadn't forgotten, though! Who was it? Who could even have information like this? Olivia felt it was equally important to find the author of the note as it was to investigate this story.

She stared both at the note and at the article in front of her now. Could Amanda's death have been a repeat of the horrible event, taken place so long ago? Was Jack responsible? Was something buried in Jack that surfaced once again, something that could not be extinguished? And who was the person who wanted this information to be known? Who had something against Jack?

Olivia jumped up and raced to her phone and dialed. She knew without doubt she had to report this to the police immediately.

Although it was late, Weston picked up immediately.

"You're still up?" was the first thing he said when he heard Olivia's voice.

"You're still up, too?" she answered.

"I'm still at the station," Weston responded. "What's up?"

"I have an anonymous note that was slipped into my room," Olivia quickly responded.

"Really?" Weston listened intently.

"The note's written by hand," Olivia elaborated. "It suggests that I check into Jack's past. And into a woman named Lorna Dempsey."

"Lorna Dempsey?" Weston was rolling the name over in his mind, trying to place it.

"I've been on the computer ever since I found this," Olivia went on hurriedly.

"Why doesn't that surprise me?" asked Weston.

"Lorna Dempsey also went missing twenty years ago," Olivia continued quickly. "And she was on a tour that Jack led into the swamp."

"Really?" Weston was startled.

"The circumstances are too similar to be overlooked," Olivia responded.

"You're right," he said, slowly. "It's definitely strange, if nothing else. And the note is even stranger. You've got to give it to us so we can run a handwriting analysis on it. I'd like to know who wrote this and slipped it under your door. They're also obviously fully aware of you and your whereabouts."

"Yes, they are," said Olivia.

"Not good," Weston muttered. "The real concern here might even be the one who wrote the letter, not Jack."

"Might be," Olivia agreed.

"Okay, that's great work again," said Weston. "I'll tell Mike first thing in the morning and I'm sure they'll bring Jack back for questioning. I'll let you know exactly what happens. And for now take extra care, keep your door carefully locked. And please, it's late. Go to sleep."

"I can't," said Olivia, "my mind is racing."

"You have to," Weston replied. "Remember what I said about obsession! It will do you in, every time."

"I do remember," said Olivia, smiling. "But it seems like you're just as obsessed as me. You're bringing up the same point over and over."

Weston laughed unexpectedly. "Okay, you got me. I confess. Now, go to sleep."

*

First thing in the morning, Weston let Olivia know that Mike wanted to see the note immediately, and was calling Jack in to question him further about it. Mike also wanted to see the articles Olivia had found about Jack.

These guys are good, thought Olivia. They're on top of everything and she appreciated that. "I'll bring everything right in," she offered.

"Great," said Weston. "We need them right away."

*

By the time Olivia arrived at the station, Jack was there already in the outside corridor, waiting to be questioned. Mike and Weston then came out together to greet her.

"You guys don't lose any time, do you?" said Olivia.

"There's no time to lose," Mike reminded her, as they walked back into the main office. "As soon as the results are in from the coroner, we may be looking at a possible homicide. All tracks have to be covered. It's interesting that this note popped up just as the body was found."

"Where did it come from?" asked Olivia.

"We'll find that out pretty soon, as well," Mike added. "It's got to be covered with fingerprints and DNA. That and our handwriting analysis will take us straight to the writer. Why didn't he or she tell us about this sooner? Why was this the perfect moment to turn all eyes on Jack?"

Weston nodded forcefully then.

"I've known Jack forever and this is the first time something like this has come up. It doesn't make sense," Mike continued, disturbed by the turn of events.

"By suggesting we look into Jack the writer of the note could be deflecting attention from themselves," Weston suggested.

"Just what I was thinking," Mike agreed. "It always stinks when someone does something anonymously. What are they hiding? Why don't they just come forward?"

"Let's take this step by step," said Weston. "Call Jack in now."

Jack was called, and he walked in accompanied by an officer.

"Sit down here, Jack," Mike said warmly. The two of them clearly knew one another.

"What's this all about?" Jack looked puzzled. "I heard you got the body finally. Does this have something to do with that?"

"Not exactly." Mike shook his head. It seemed hard for him to go forward with this, but of course, he knew he had to. "Some slipped a weird note under Olivia's door last night," he started.

Jack looked confused. "So, what's that got to do with me?"

"The note mentioned you," Mike continued. "It told Olivia to check on your past. Especially what happened to Lorna Dempsey."

"Lorna Dempsey?" Jack was utterly amazed. "That's past history. It must have happened at least twenty years ago."

"Yes, that's right," Mike continued in a low voice. "Olivia checked and found out that Lorna went missing on one of your tours, too. It happened in the same spot as Amanda, almost."

Jack began to look strange. "So what does that add up to? Lorna was a completely different situation. There was a storm with big winds and the boats then were different. She was blown off the side into the water. We tried our best to get her, but couldn't. She was never found again."

"I know, I know." Mike tried to calm the situation.

"They brought me in for questioning then and it amounted to nothing, of course." Jack's voice got louder. "What's the reason for bringing this up now?"

"That's the real question, isn't it?" said Weston.

"Someone's got it in for me?" Jack looked amazed.

"Big time," said Mike, confidentially.

Jack began to fume. "Who the hell wrote this note?"

"That's what we're going to find out," Mike assured him.

"You just let me know who wrote it the minute you find out." Jack wasn't taking this well at the moment.

"No worries." Mike clearly wanted to brush it under the carpet and Olivia didn't like that.

"I'm not worried, I'm mad," Jack answered.

"Don't sweat it." Mike's voice got louder. "There are all kinds of nuts around looking for attention, you know that."

"But what they found is interesting, isn't it?" Olivia tried to stay on track. So far no one had asked Jack for further details about the story. They just accepted it as it was. Olivia was curious to find out more.

"What's interesting about it?" Jack turned on Olivia now. "People die, honey, they disappear, get caught in storms and wrecks all over. We're used to that down in the glades."

Jack was clearly trying to halt any probing into what had happened with Lorna.

"Lorna Dempsey wasn't wearing a life vest or something to protect her in case of a storm?" Olivia went forward.

Jack's face got red. "What are you implying? That I don't protect my customers? That I lead them into trouble? That there's something wrong with my tours? I wouldn't suggest something like that if I were you. I'm known in these parts and respected. If someone wants to take me down, they'll have to wrestle with a whole lot of folks who are on my team. I wouldn't like to see something like that happen."

Jack was trying to intimidate Olivia, obviously feeling threatened by the news. But Olivia didn't like his reaction. If he was completely innocent why would he behave this way?

Weston quickly intervened. "No one's trying to take you down, Jack," he insisted, "least of all Olivia. She's just doing her job. Someone slipped the note to her."

"Well, find out who wrote it and slipped it under her door," Jack agreed. "That's the person who's after me! I need to know exactly who."

Mike and Weston nodded. Then they both stood up to signify the interview with Jack was over.

"You can go now," Mike offered. "Thanks for coming in. I just wanted to see there was anything you might want to add."

"Nothing plus nothing equals nothing," Jack said. "I'm glad you brought me in though. It's important to know that someone out there's against me."

"We'll keep you informed of whatever we find," Mike replied.

"I know you will, buddy," said Jack as the office phone rang loudly.

Weston went right over to pick it up. "Hello," he said and then grew silent. "Wait a minute! You're kidding me!"

"What is it?" Mike stepped closer to him.

"I don't believe this." Weston was enrapt.

"Tell me!" Mike insisted.

Weston put his hand over the speaker. "It's the coroner's office," he declared. "The remains don't belong to Amanda!"

"What?" Mike looked like he was about to fall over.

"The remains belong to someone else. Another young woman, named Lilly Feld."

"Lilly who?" Mike was beside himself.

"Do you have a missing person's case like that open?" Olivia jumped right in.

"No we don't." Mike was certain of it.

"She could be listed missing in another county," Weston suggested.

"All the counties share the listings. We would have heard of her," Mike replied.

"Maybe no one even knew she was gone?" said Olivia. "Could she have been down here alone?"

"Could she, would she? This can go on forever," said Jack. "Right now all I care about is finding the person who sent that letter to Olivia!"

"Oh God, we're back to a missing person's investigation now with Amanda," Mike breathed. "Hold on a minute, Jack, you've got to tell us more."

Jack looked appalled. "You're gonna make trouble for me just because of a crazy accident twenty years ago?"

"Of course not," Mike answered. "We just need to find some trace of Amanda ASAP. You know the swamp like the back of your hand."

"Sure I do," Jack responded. "And it knows me. What has that got to do with finding Amanda?"

"You tell us! Where in the world can she be?" Weston chimed in.

"If I knew, don't you think I'd tell you?" asked Jack, incredulously. "You think I have something to do with her disappearance?"

"Of course not," Mike uttered. "But somebody knows where she is right now."

"You're grabbing at straws," Jack answered. "Who in the hell really knows what goes on in the swamp?"

*

Amanda's case turned back into a missing person, and an investigation into what happened to Lilly Feld opened simultaneously.

"These two cases may have nothing to do with one another," the news blasted, "or maybe they have. Anyone with information about Lilly Feld is being asked to call the police immediately. Did the women know one another? Did their paths ever cross?"

CHAPTER THIRTEEN

Olivia left the station disturbed by Jack's behavior. Something didn't sit right and she was determined to find out more. There was no way she would leave a stone unturned if there was even the slightest possibility that Amanda was still alive. As Olivia walked along the breezy streets of Key Largo, she thought about what to do next. It was disturbing that the police were only focusing upon the person who wrote the note and letting Jack off scot-free. Why were they closing ranks around him? Jack was certainly an established figure in these parts. Would there be trouble for the police if they didn't get behind him?

As Olivia walked her phone rang, and she picked up, expecting more news from Weston. To her surprise, Wayne was on the other end.

"How's it going?" he asked as soon as Olivia answered. "The case is all over the news, the only thing everyone's talking about."

Olivia was happy to hear from Wayne again. "You can say that again," she replied, "the case has caught fire. It's up and down and then up again."

"That's putting it mildly," said Wayne. "What a strange turn of events."

"You mean that the remains didn't belong to Amanda? That we still only have a missing person's case?" Olivia asked.

"Yes," Wayne replied. "You guys had everyone fooled. We thought for sure you'd found Amanda."

"I thought that too, mostly," Olivia replied.

"Mostly?" asked Wayne.

"There's still a part of me that holds out hope," Olivia continued, "as crazy as it seems."

"Holding out hope is never crazy," Wayne quickly replied. "What do we have left when hope is gone? Nothing. It's hard to move forward then."

Olivia closed her eyes. It felt good to hear it. "I also just received an odd handwritten note," she went on. "Whoever wrote it didn't sign it, just told me to check into Jack. He's the guy who owns the tour company. And it also added a name, Lorna Dempsey."

"Who's Lorna Dempsey?" Wayne was glued to the story.

"She's a woman who went missing on one of Jack's tours twenty years ago. It was looked into then and the police have just finished questioning him about it again now. It all seems to amount to nothing," Olivia added.

"Nothing amounts to nothing," said Wayne, forcefully. "There's a reason someone wanted to get that note to you."

"The police are mainly focusing on the person who could have sent it," she added.

"That's important," Wayne agreed, "but I'd say the main focus should be on Jack."

"Lorna Dempsey drowned in the swamp right where Amanda went missing," Olivia continued. "No charges were ever pressed."

"That's too much of a coincidence. It's definitely not nothing," Wayne added intensely.

"Jack got really defensive when I pushed further," Olivia went on. "He actually tried to intimidate me."

"I'm seeing red flags everywhere," Wayne reacted. "You go check further into Jack. When they start to bully, they've usually got something to hide."

"That's exactly what I thought," said Olivia. "I've checked already and he comes up clean. He's a respected person in the glades. And no matter what we've asked him, he adamantly denies knowing anything more."

"Then follow the money trail." Wayne's voice dropped, confidentially. "That always leads just where you need to go."

Olivia appreciated Wayne's intelligent, measured ways. "It's great to talk to you," she said without hesitation. "And I like your idea."

"It's always great to talk to you, too," he replied. "Go get a forensic accountant immediately. They have a way of digging out the truth fast."

"What exactly would he be looking for?" asked Olivia. "Crooked dealings?"

"He'll look for anything he can find," answered Wayne. "It's a fishing expedition, basically. You never know what will come up."

"Thanks so much, Wayne," Olivia repeated.

"It's my pleasure, always," he replied. "And keep in touch, please. Call me! And remember, you're not in this alone."

Olivia smiled at Wayne's request. She was about to tell him that she didn't feel alone, that Weston had been assigned to her as a point person on the force. But suddenly, she refrained. There was no reason to go on about Weston. Weston and Wayne were entirely

75

different, with almost opposing points of views. It was fascinating to have both of them on board. Olivia learned a lot from both of them.

"Thanks again, Wayne," Olivia said. "We'll talk again soon, I promise."

After Olivia hung up, she thought about Wayne's suggestions more deeply. The idea of digging deeper into Jack's finances was smart. It was also a great idea to get a forensic accountant on the case. Maybe Jack was right. Maybe someone was against him. If so, this might help find out why. After all, there definitely was a reason someone had sent her the note. Olivia needed a professional check to be done immediately.

*

Olivia cleared the idea with Mike first. To her relief, he liked it and without any delay gave her the name of Burt, a top forensic accountant.

"I need results ASAP," Olivia said to Burt the minute she met him in his office nearby. "There's no time to lose. For all we know, there's even a possibility Amanda could still be alive."

Burt, a solid, hefty guy, looked at Olivia out of the corner of his eye.

"Sure," he agreed, "anything's possible. I'm on it immediately. You'll have an answer in the blink of an eye."

"Thanks so much," said Olivia, "and I'll keep checking on Jack as well."

Olivia went back to her hotel room then and dove into her computer fiercely. Avidly, she checked through every little thing she could find on Jack. But wherever she looked, he came up smelling like roses. Jack was involved in one civic movement after another, seemed to be the perfect citizen. As the long afternoon grew to a close, Olivia's hope of finding anything suspicious on Jack faded away.

Just as she was about to close her computer, to her delight, her phone rang. Could it be Wayne, checking to see if Olivia had followed his suggestion and was on the money trail?

She picked up quickly, and to her surprise, Burt was on the other end.

"I've got something here," Burt said quickly.

Olivia was startled. "Already?"

Burt laughed. "It wasn't hard to find, came up immediately."

"What was it?" Olivia was thrilled.

"Just before Amanda and Tye came down here for their vacation, Tye wired a large sum of money to Jack."

"What?" Olivia was startled. "For what purpose?"

"That's the question, isn't it?" Burt replied.

"I had no idea that they even knew each other," Olivia mentioned.

"They definitely had contact with one another before the couple arrived," Burt repeated.

"Irregular?" Olivia questioned.

"I'd definitely say so," Burt agreed. "Certainly worth looking into further. In fact, you have to. Right away."

"Thanks so much," breathed Olivia. "I'll do that right away."

*

Olivia put a call in to Tye instantly, but he didn't pick up. She left a quick message asking him to call her and wondered where he might be. Then she remembered Tye had a couple of friends down here now. He was probably out with them somewhere.

Olivia texted immediately. ***Where are you, Tye? Something has just come up and it's urgent that we talk again. Text me back to let me know you got this.***

Olivia waited a few minutes for a reply. It didn't come. He's probably at his hotel, she thought, annoyed that he hadn't answered. Best to go over and see for myself.

*

Without saying a word to anyone, Olivia went straight to Tye's hotel and asked at the front desk for him. The woman there looked at Olivia nervously.

"I have no idea where he is," she replied. "I haven't seen him in a while."

"That's unusual, isn't it?" Olivia pursued it.

"Not at all," the woman replied. "People come and go all the time."

"But don't you usually see him around?" Olivia didn't let it go.

"Sometimes, but why? Should I?" The woman looked confused.

Olivia decided to go straight up to Tye's room then and knock on the door herself. Perhaps he was sleeping and hadn't gotten her messages. Or perhaps he was somewhere else. The police had told him to stay close to the hotel in case something came up. He'd been good about it up to now. They'd always been able to reach him.

It was probably a good idea to call Weston first, Olivia thought, and see if he knew what Tye was up to. After all, Tye might be just a few steps away, for all she knew.

"I'm trying to locate Tye," Olivia said to Weston as soon as he picked up.

"Why do you want to locate him for?" Weston was surprised.

"It's important for me to talk to him further," was all Olivia was ready to say.

"I get that," Weston answered. "But it's been really rough for Tye these past few days. He's probably somewhere in town with his friends. I'm glad they finally came down."

"But he's supposed to stay at the hotel, isn't he?" Olivia objected.

"It's true," Weston agreed, "but he's not under house arrest. He's actually not even a person of interest. Right now the guy's just a grieving husband and you've got to cut him some slack."

But Olivia didn't want to cut Tye slack. She kept thinking of what Irma had told her about him and his marriage. She also didn't want to get into it with Weston now.

"Has his room been checked out by the police?" Olivia went on.

"No, not at all." Weston got quiet. "Why? Did you find something on him? If you did then we would check out his room."

"I'm not sure yet," Olivia answered.

Weston didn't like any of this. "Well, let me know as soon as you do," he said. "And until you do, please give the guy some slack. He needs it." Then he quickly hung up the phone.

Olivia knew she'd found something on Tye, but wasn't sure exactly what it meant yet. It was too soon to spread it around. She was determined to get into Tye's room, though, and have a quick look around.

Olivia immediately took the elevator up and knocked on the door.

No answer. Maybe Weston was right, maybe she should back off. Tye could be out taking a walk and getting some air. There was no reason to assume anything worse.

After knocking again and getting no answer, Olivia paused and wondered what to do. She certainly had just cause to enter the room and simply look around. What would be wrong with that if it helped bring Amanda home?

Without hesitating another moment, Olivia put her hand on the knob, turned, and pushed the door in. It opened a crack, but not enough for her to get in. There had to be a way, though. She just wanted to look around for a few moments, scan everything with her own eyes.

Fortunately, at that moment, a waiter came out of the elevator wheeling a cart of food to another room on the floor.

Olivia was all over it. "So great to see you," she said to him. "I'm Detective Olivia Wells. I've just gotten a call and need to get into this room immediately."

The waiter looked startled, then afraid. "Is this about the case of that missing woman?" he sputtered.

"Exactly," said Olivia hurriedly. "The door just needs an extra push. Do you have something on the tray that could help me? We don't have time to waste."

The waiter looked startled and nervous again. "I'm not sure I should do this," he answered.

"It'll just take a second," said Olivia, pulling out her identification from her bag and showing it to him. "Time's of the essence and the door's almost open as it is."

The waiter accompanied her to the door then and tried to open it naturally. "You're right, it's almost open," he said as he took a knife from the tray and slipped it gently into a crack in the lock. The door immediately flew open then.

"Thanks so much, I really appreciate this," said Olivia. "You did a good thing. You're helping everyone."

"I'm glad I did. No problem," said the waiter, grabbing his tray and pushing it further down the hall.

Olivia quickly slipped into Tye's room, looking around for anything she could find. It was a weird stroke of luck that he wasn't here now, she thought. And it was certainly a stroke of luck that the waiter had come along exactly when he did.

Tye's room was neat and orderly, with just a few magazines sprawled over the couch. Olivia went to the bureau along the wall and began opening one drawer after another. Everything was stacked in perfect order inside. Olivia lifted a few piles of clothing in one drawer and quickly looked around. Nothing there. She then shut that drawer and looked in another. She had no idea what she was looking for, but kept going anyhow. Something might pop out at her. You never knew.

Suddenly, in the last drawer on the bottom, Olivia spotted a blue velvet box, hidden in a corner. Startled, she looked at the box for a long time, then reached over and lifted it out.

Olivia opened the velvet box carefully. She gasped when she saw a huge diamond ring inside.

"What's this?" she said to no one at all. Olivia's thoughts starting racing. Tye and Amanda were married already. Who was this engagement ring for? And what was it doing here inside his drawer?

The diamond ring glittered up at Olivia, disturbing her further. Could the ring possibly belong to Amanda? If so, what was it doing here hidden in the back of Tye's drawer? Or was it a ring Tye was planning to give his wife? If so, why hadn't he done it by now? Then another possibility hit Olivia. The ring was waiting here for someone else. Tye had been waiting to give it to another woman after Amanda was finally gone!

Olivia stared at the ring for a long moment. This ring could be the key that would finally crack the case open. Tye was secretly involved with another woman, somewhere close by. A huge chill swept over Olivia at the thought. It made the most sense of all.

CHAPTER FOURTEEN

Without waiting another moment, Olivia immediately put a call in to Weston.

"I found something," she announced breathlessly, "and I've got to speak to Tye immediately."

"He's still not at the hotel?" Weston answered fast.

"Not that I know of," Olivia replied. "I don't see him and he's not in his room."

"Where are you?" Weston sounded startled. "At his hotel?"

"Yes, I came by to see him," said Olivia.

"Okay, wait a second, I'll get you an answer," Weston replied promptly.

Olivia waited for what seemed like forever for Weston to jump back on the other end of the phone.

"Nobody knows exactly where Tye is now," Weston reported, "but there's a club in town, the Wanderers. Go to the club in a couple of hours and most likely you'll find Weston there."

"What's he doing at a club when his wife is missing?" Olivia couldn't help but ask.

"Come on, Olivia." Weston wasn't pleased. "What's the guy supposed to do? Never leave his room? Just sit there and drive himself crazy? I told you already, cut him some slack. What did you find out about him anyway?"

"I'll tell you when I see you in person," Olivia replied. "Who told you he would be at the Wanderers?"

"I'll tell you that later as well," Weston remarked.

Weston was great about many things. When things came to a boiling point, he'd jump right in. He was tight-lipped, though, held a lot close to the vest. Wayne was exactly the opposite of that.

"Anyway, go to the club in a couple of hours," Weston repeated.

"Got it," Olivia answered succinctly. "Thanks so much for finding out about it."

"No problem," Weston replied, sounding doubtful that Olivia would find much of anything at the club at all.

*

81

The Wanderers was a local club in Key Largo, situated down near the water under a cluster of old palm trees. The club featured a live jazz band, a garden in the back, dancing, drinks, and good company.

Olivia walked inside, dressed in a short, black sleeveless dress, her hair loose around her face. Lots of eyes turned as she entered and Olivia smiled to notice that there was no shortage of interested guys. She'd forgotten about this part of life, being out and about, having a good time, meeting guys and dating. For a moment she missed it all. She missed being just another woman who wanted the normal things of life. Then Olivia stopped and thought about Amanda. Amanda had been married, had all the good things that life could bring. And where was she now? What had happened to her happiness? Olivia paused and took it all in. A life dedicated to finding Amanda and others who'd fallen into terrible traps seemed the best life Olivia could imagine.

Olivia immediately decided to forget the guys at the bar and turn her attention back to finding Tye. She scanned the bar to see if he was there. The light was dim and it was hard to make anything out exactly. Olivia saw a tall, lanky bartender with a friendly face and upbeat manner close by, watching her. She moved a few steps closer to him.

"Looking for someone?" the bartender asked.

"Is Tye Fisher here, by any chance?" asked Olivia.

You mean the guy whose wife went missing?" The bartender became alert.

"Yes," she answered.

"Tye's usually down there at the end of the bar with a couple of his friends," the bartender said. "Lousy luck he's had for sure."

"Terrible," Olivia agreed.

"And he's taking it hard, too," the bartender added. "If I ever saw a crushed guy, it's him."

"Sorry about that, so sorry," Olivia added as she turned and walked away, trying to find Tye.

At the very end of the bar a young man was sitting on the stool, leaning over the bar. Two other young men hovered around him. That had to be him, Olivia thought, as she walked right over.

"Tye?" Olivia asked as she approached.

The guy leaning over the bar straightened up and the two young men around him turned toward her.

"Yeah, it's Tye," one of his friends answered. "Who are you?"

"Olivia Wells. Detective on the case," she responded.

Tye spun around and looked up at Olivia. How long had he been drinking? His face was puffy, his eyes blurry and unfocused.

"Greetings," he mumbled, slurring his words. "Fancy meeting you here."

"What's this about?" one of his friends asked quickly.

"Tye and I know each other," Olivia started. "I just wanted to talk to him for a few minutes now."

"It's fine." Tye motioned his friends to the side and got up from the stool, weaving as he stood. He seemed pleased to see Olivia, though, which surprised her.

"Can we have a few minutes alone out in the back garden?" Olivia asked him lightly.

"Sure," said Tye.

"What's it about? What is it?" the friend demanded.

"It's okay, Phil." Tye calmed him down. "It has to be about Amanda and I want to hear what Olivia has to say."

"More bad news?" The friend seemed agitated.

"No, not exactly," Olivia reassured him.

"Let's go." Tye was eager.

Grateful, Olivia led him away out to the back garden, which had many empty benches under trees. This was the perfect spot to sit down and talk.

"Thanks for talking to me, Tye," Olivia said, as they sat down.

"Sure, sure," he mumbled. "I've actually been thinking of you and the force. You're all doing your best."

"We are," agreed Olivia. "But we're back to square one again now."

"Yeah." Tye nodded. "And now someone else has been killed down here, too. It makes things complicated."

Olivia shivered. "What do you mean, *killed too*?" She picked up on it immediately.

"I'm talking about that lady whose remains were found in the alligator," Tye replied.

"You said, *killed too*, though!" Olivia repeated. "Do you feel that Amanda was killed?"

"Could be? I don't know anymore." Tye put his head in his hands.

"Tye." Olivia needed him to stay alert and talk to her. She decided to shock him with more news she'd found.

"What?" He looked up at her sadly.

"I found an engagement ring hidden in your bureau," she whispered.

Olivia's plan worked. Tye was shocked, his eyes flying open. "You found what?"

"I found a diamond ring in a blue velvet box hidden in your drawer," Olivia repeated.

"Okay, so what?" he finally said.

"What was it doing there? Who's it for?" Olivia didn't hold back.

"I got it for Amanda," Tye said in a voice that grew rougher. "I was planning to propose to her all over again."

"Really? That's odd," said Olivia.

"Nothing odd about it." Tye's voice had a sharp edge now. "This was our anniversary weekend and I was determined to start over and make things right this time."

"I thought you said things were great, though." Olivia didn't buy it.

"Things were great at first." Tye's eyes opened wider. "Then they went downhill, fast."

"You didn't mention that before." Olivia kept prodding.

"Why should I?" A combative tone entered Tye's voice. "There was no reason to embarrass her or me. So I told you now. I was determined to make things perfect again! So I bought her the big ring she always wanted."

"Amanda doesn't sound like someone who would care about the size of her ring," Olivia couldn't help comment.

"Well, you're wrong there. She cared very much!" Tye shot back. Amanda was always unhappy with the ring I got her, kept telling me it was too small. She said it over and over. There wasn't a week I didn't hear about it. So, for our anniversary, I went down to Key West and bought her this rock. I was planning to give it to her over the weekend."

"But she disappeared first," Olivia whispered.

"That's right, she did," Tye breathed. "And when she comes back I'll give her the ring."

Olivia looked at him hard. She wasn't sure if it was the alcohol that was making him speak, or something else.

"What went wrong in your marriage?" Olivia asked, intensely.

"I wouldn't say something went wrong," Tye muttered then.

"You just did though." Olivia brought him back to focus.

"I would say it was trouble waiting to happen all along," Tye muttered. "Deep down Amanda was a wild one. And she hid it pretty good. When we were dating she held everything together and just focused on getting us to tie the knot. Once we got married, different sides of her started coming out fast."

84

Olivia realized how common that was. "What sides of her did you see?" she asked.

"I told you, Amanda was a wild one," Tye repeated. "No one imagined how wild, either. She wanted one adventure after another."

"What kind of adventure?" Olivia needed him to be very specific.

"She wanted to go on vacations almost every weekend," Tye muttered. "She kept scheduling parties and events for us to attend all week long. Enough was never enough for her."

"Was it too much for you?" asked Olivia.

"I wasn't raised that way," Tye answered. "My mother respected my father. He made the plans and she went along. But Amanda wanted to run the show." Tye rubbed his foot on the soil below.

"Things didn't fit well between you?" Olivia kept him talking.

"We definitely had to work things out," Tye murmured. "That's not so different from any other couple, though, is it? "

It was a good question. "It depends how much has to be worked out," said Olivia. "Sometimes it's too much, can't be done. Sometimes you've just chosen the wrong partner."

Tye looked upset by her comment. While he was feeling vulnerable, Olivia knew she had to shake him further. Who knew what he'd tell her then?

"You also wired a large sum of money to Jack Healey, the guy who owns the touring company, didn't you?" Olivia turned up the heat.

Tye sobered up quickly and rubbed his foot harder back and forth.

"You're really closing in on me, aren't you?" he muttered.

"Not closing in, checking everything out carefully. I have to," Olivia replied.

"I wired Jack the money to make sure he'd give us extra attention and do us a favor," Tye finally said.

"What favor?" asked Olivia.

"Amanda really wanted to go further into the swamp on the tour. She'd checked it out and found where the tour ended. But she was desperate to go a few extra steps. She was like that, always pushed the edges. So I sent Jack a nice bonus to make sure it happened."

"Why was it so important for her to go further into the swamp?" asked Olivia.

85

"I just told you, if she didn't push the edge, she wasn't happy." Tye's face contorted as his voice grew threatening. "Why did she want to do it? Because she wanted to, plain and simple. And I had to give her whatever she wanted or there'd be hell to pay! In fact, that's why I planned to propose to her again and give her this damn ring. I thought it would make her happy and we could finally have a new start."

Olivia was stunned by the story. It gave her an entirely different picture of Amanda. But could she believe it? There were pieces that didn't fit.

"But even though it was so important to her, you never went on the tour at all," Olivia added.

"No, as luck had it, I couldn't," Tye answered fast. "I woke up feeling lousy that morning, nauseous and vomiting. How could I go out into the swamp feeling like that?"

"You couldn't," Olivia agreed, wondering how much of this was Tye's imagination. Had he concocted this story ahead of time to cover the loopholes? It seemed strangely convenient that Tye hadn't been able to go out on the tour that day, after such careful preparation.

"That's all I've got to say." Tye stood up then, still weaving. "I feel lousy today."

"Wait a minute." Olivia got up as well and put her hand on his arm to steady him.

"Wait for what?" Tye turned on her, irritated. "Wait for someone else to turn up dead in an alligator's mouth?"

It was a horrible image and Olivia shuddered.

"I want to ask you one more thing," she shot back, but Tye immediately charged away, quickly jolting back into the bar,

Olivia sat there alone for a few moments. She felt as if she'd just had an encounter with a chameleon. There were many pieces of Tye's story that had to be validated. The police could check with Jack about the money Tye had wired into his account. Would Jack confirm the purpose of it? And Olivia still wasn't sure what to believe about the ring. Tye said he'd bought it in Key West. She'd have to look into that, as well. Why Key West? What was he doing down there, anyway?

Sitting out in the garden, Olivia could hear the noise in the club growing louder and more raucous. It was probably filling up as the night went on. Olivia wondered if it was okay to go back to her hotel now. Was there anything else for her to find here?

As she sat there pondering, to Olivia's surprise, two young women rushed out into the back garden, right over to her.

"Olivia, remember me?" It was Irma.

"Of course I do." Olivia was startled to see her.

"This is Dale, another good friend of Amanda's." Irma quickly introduced the young woman beside her. "Dale and I came here to talk to Tye and one of his friends said he was outside in the garden, talking to you."

"That's right," said Olivia.

"I don't know what he told you," Irma went on, "but I want to say something, too."

"Please go ahead." Olivia was ready for anything.

"Dale and I were horrified when we thought Amanda's remains were found," Irma continued. "Just horrified."

"I can only imagine," said Olivia.

"And Tye's a great talker, but don't believe everything he tells you," Irma said.

Olivia remembered that there was bad blood between Tye and Irma.

"What exactly did he tell you tonight?" Irma was probing.

"Whatever he said is totally confidential, of course." Olivia stopped her.

Irma didn't like that, backed off a little.

"What is it you want to tell me, though?" Olivia added.

For the moment Irma had nothing else to say.

Dale stepped forward. "Tye spends quite a bit of time down in the Keys, regularly," she offered. "We thought you should know that. He even comes down here alone without Amanda, quite often."

"Why?" asked Olivia, interested.

"He has customers down here," Irma joined in. "He's designing a house in Key West for someone. That's as good an excuse as any to get away a lot."

Irma definitely had it in for Tye and Olivia was intrigued by it. She was also interested to see how much Irma knew about the details of Amanda's personal life.

"Did Amanda tell you that about Tye?" asked Olivia.

"Yes, she did," Irma retorted, "but it's common knowledge that he comes to the Keys all the time."

This was information that Olivia was glad to have. It answered part of her question about why Tye had bought the ring in Key West. But only part.

"Listen, we have to go now." Irma began tugging Dale's arm. "I was just hoping you'd give me a real update." Irma flashed

87

Olivia an irritated glance. "But I guess I'm not part of the inner circle and everything you know is super confidential!"

"When I'm able to give you more information, I certainly will," Olivia answered professionally. "And, of course, some information is confidential. I'm not purposely holding anything back."

"Of course you aren't." Dale pulled her arm away from Irma. "Thanks so much for all your efforts, Olivia. Please call us any time at all we can be of help."

"I will," answered Olivia, as Dale leaned over and handed Olivia her card, slyly.

*

Time was running out for sure and Amanda knew it. She'd been feeling weaker and weaker the last day. It was harder to breathe and she was sleepy. She couldn't give in, she wouldn't. The past day he'd stopped bringing her water to drink and sat over there in the corner sulking. When she'd begged for food or water, he hadn't paid any attention either, almost as if he didn't hear a thing. Amanda had stopped pleading and lay down on the damp ground to conserve every inch of her energy. Even though her body was limp, her mind was sharper than ever, fine-tuned. She could hear the least little flutter of a bird's wing rustling out there in the trees.

In the dim light coming in through the tiny window, Amanda now turned and saw his eyes glaring at her, hating her, wanting to end this. Why didn't he? What was stopping him from taking her life as he'd threatened over and over? Why was he curled up there, immovable? Both of them immovable. How come?

CHAPTER FIFTEEN

First thing the next morning Olivia went to the station to go over the details of what she'd found with Weston and Mike. The two of them were sitting at a long table drinking coffee and eating muffins. Once Olivia started talking they put down their coffee cups and listened intently.

"Buying another engagement ring for your wife is definitely irregular," Mike agreed, when Olivia showed it to them.

"That's some rock," said Weston, amazed. "Looks like he was buttering her up."

"Buttering her up to keep the peace?" asked Olivia. "Seems Amanda was giving him a hard time."

"Really?" Weston looked uncomfortable.

"That's a pretty expensive price to pay for peace, though." Mike didn't buy it. "Most guys wouldn't do it. This ring has to be something more than that.

"Tye also did his best to get away from Amanda often," Olivia continued. "Seems he spent a lot of time in the Keys. He actually bought the ring in Key West."

"Interesting," Mike murmured.

"Frankly," Olivia continued, "I'm not sure who the ring was really for."

"What are you talking about?" Weston was startled.

"Does Tye have someone else down here he bought the ring for? Did Amanda find out about it? Was that woman responsible for what happened to Amanda?" Olivia blasted out one idea after another.

"That's all wild conjecture." Weston was agitated. "There's nothing that points to it at all."

"Shouldn't we look into it, though?" asked Olivia.

"You can dream up a thousand scenarios and spend your whole life looking into them," Weston shot back. "But there's no evidence pointing to the ideas you've presented!"

"Tye and Amanda were unhappy," Olivia disagreed. "They were trying to patch up a bad relationship. It's possible he got involved with someone else."

"Anything is possible," Mike agreed. "But there's no evidence pointing to it, is there? Anything else you have for us?"

Both Mike and Weston were minimizing the ring, thought Olivia. They didn't want to go down that path. But, thankfully, she had more for them.

"I've also discovered that Tye wired a sizable amount of money into Jack Healey's bank account," Olivia continued.

That really struck Mike. "What the hell are you talking about?"

"You're sure about that?" Weston cringed.

"Very sure. I followed the money trail," said Olivia. "When I asked Tye about it, he said he wired the money to make sure Jack gave him and Amanda special treatment on the tour. He wanted Jack to let Amanda go further out into the swamp. It was what she wanted."

At that both Mike and Weston sprang into action. "Okay, we're on it," said Mike. "I'll check that story with Jack immediately."

"And Olivia should go down to Key West immediately," Weston added. "Let's find the name of the jeweler who sold Tye the ring. It would be good for Olivia to speak to him in person. It's possible Tye told the jeweler who or what the ring was for. Olivia can also get the jeweler's impression of both Tye and his purchase."

The idea of going to Key West pleased Olivia. And she was glad Mike would check the financial transaction immediately.

Mike looked disturbed by the turn of events, though. "Once I talk to Jack and Olivia reports back from Key West, it will give us all a better idea if any foul play could be at work here," he continued. "If not, we can just finish it up. We can say that Amanda came upon hard times in the swamp. She went further than she should have."

Olivia was agitated by the idea of closing the case, wasn't about to let that happen. "But we have no idea that's what happened to her."

"No one does," snapped Weston. "But when a case is closed after careful investigation you take the most likely possibility."

"I don't believe Amanda's disappearance had anything to do with the swamp." Olivia was steadfast. "The glades are a wonderful setting to camouflage what really happened!"

"Could be," Mike agreed, "but it's unlikely."

And I still feel Amanda's alive," Olivia couldn't help saying.

"Still alive?" Mike was dumbfounded.

"Oh brother." Weston shook his head.

Mike tried to calm things down. "Let's just take this one step at a time now," he cautioned. "You go to Key West, Olivia, and I'll get right in touch with Jack."

*

Olivia took the next flight down to Key West. It would be arriving in no time. On the plane she put a quick call into Wayne to let him know she was arriving.

To her delight he picked up immediately. "I'm calling from the plane to Key West," Olivia said right away.

"Really?" Wayne sounded surprised.

"There's someone I've got to talk to in Key West," said Olivia.

"Well, that's lucky for me," said Wayne. "I'm glad you'll be around."

"Me, too," said Olivia.

"Are you up for our long overdue dinner tonight?" Wayne went on. "I don't imagine you'll be staying long."

Olivia smiled; he hadn't forgotten about their missed dinner. She liked that. Wayne was also aware that time was tight. No pressure.

"Tonight would be great," Olivia answered. "You're right, I'm in and out fast."

"Wonderful," said Wayne. "I'll pick you up at six. Does that work?"

"It does," said Olivia. Her plane back to Key Largo wasn't until eight, and it would be nice seeing Wayne again. Olivia was actually surprised at how good it felt to be returning to Key West right now. It was even beginning to feel like home.

The plane arrived in no time and Olivia was back in her apartment before she knew it. Weston had set up an appointment for her with the jeweler for an hour from now. She quickly showered, changed, and looked things over in the apartment. To her surprise, everything was just as she'd left it. Except, Olivia wasn't the same. Each day she was different. She grew, she changed. Even now she was someone different from who she was when she'd left for Key Largo.

In a few moments, Olivia left the apartment and grabbed a cab to the jewelry store where Tye had purchased the ring. The store owner, Edmond Tapp, was expecting her and Olivia wanted to be right on time.

The moment she walked into the store, a well-dressed middle-aged man walked toward her.

"You must be Olivia Wells," he said immediately. "Your fame is well established."

Olivia looked at him oddly. What fame? she thought. It was an odd way to put it. He was trying to flatter her.

"I am Edmond Tapp," he continued.

"Pleased to meet you," said Olivia, deciding not to make a point of his comment.

"Please come with me, Olivia," Edmond continued with exaggerated formality. "I will show you our collection of extraordinary rings, including vintage diamonds."

"That's not necessary," said Olivia quickly, cutting through to the chase.

Edmond looked both startled and offended, and Olivia was sorry about that.

"I certainly don't mean to offend you," Olivia responded to his strange glance. "Time is short and I have to stay focused."

"Of course, I respect that." Edmond stood taller. "It's just that most women love looking at our collections."

"I'm sure they're beautiful," said Olivia. "But I'm here to talk."

Though Edmond wasn't sure what to make of that, he acquiesced.

"Please come to my office then," he continued, leading Olivia through the sleek store displaying precious jewels of all kinds. It was not the kind of store commonly found in Key West.

Edmond opened the door to a room at the side and they walked into his perfectly designed office. As Olivia took a seat she suddenly wondered if Edmond and Tye knew each other well. Could they have even been friends?

"Do you know Tye well?" Olivia started, wanted to get beneath Edmond's polished surface as quickly as possible.

"I know Tye Fisher, of course," Edmond responded.

"Are you friends?" Olivia continued.

Edmond looked put off by the question. "Not exactly friends, but certainly friendly acquaintances."

"Is Tye a regular customer, has he purchased other jewelry here?" asked Olivia.

"I meant to say that Tye and I have run into each other socially, here and there." Edmond sidestepped the question gracefully.

Olivia realized that Tye worked for wealthy people down here, designing homes. He could have certainly run into Edmond at a party. At the very least, Edmond must have come highly recommended by some of Tye's clientele.

"You and Tye both work with the same clientele, I imagine." Olivia was putting the pieces together.

"Exactly," said Edmond. "Tye is well thought of in Key West and so am I."

"Very nice," said Olivia, trying to put Edmond at ease.

"And, of course, I am unaccustomed to speaking to detectives," Edmond remarked on his own.

"I understand," said Olivia. "Of course you know all about what happened to Tye, I assume."

"I know what happened to his wife, certainly," Edmond replied. "No one is talking about anything else these days."

Olivia was struck by Edmond's precision. Talking to her, it seemed, he had his all-points-alert system on.

"Any little piece of information could possibly help us find Amanda." Olivia wanted to put their conversation in its larger context. "Even something that seems simple or unimportant."

"Are you suggesting I know something about what happened to Tye's wife?" Edmond seemed truly startled.

"You may not even realize that you know it," Olivia replied.

"Like what?" Edmond was emboldened.

"Well, for starters, I need to know about Tye's purchase of the ring," Olivia said.

"Tye paid for it entirely with cash," Edmond responded, crisply.

"That's unusual?" asked Olivia.

"It's notable," Edmond replied.

"That's very good to know," said Olivia, "but not exactly what I was wondering about."

"What do you want to know?" Edmond seemed to grow more uncomfortable as their discussion progressed.

"Why did Tye buy an engagement ring for Amanda when they're already married?"

Edmond paused and looked incredulous. "That's entirely Tye's business, isn't it?"

"Not entirely, not now," said Olivia, crisply. "Not when the ring was never given to her and she suddenly went missing."

"I'm sure he was about to give it to her," Edmond objected.

"Did Tye tell you that it was for her, exactly?" Olivia plunged into the heart of the matter.

"Yes, of course," said Edmond. "He was excited to buy it for her too. Kept asking if I thought it would suit her."

"Really? Why would he ask you that? Did you know Amanda?" Olivia was startled.

"No, I'd never met her, but he told me all about her," Edmond replied. "He said that she was beautiful, daring, loved things that were spectacular. He also mentioned that he was preparing to propose to her again this weekend. It was their anniversary."

Edmond's story backed up Tye's exactly. Almost too precisely for comfort. Olivia wondered if Tye had found out that she was going to speak to Edmond. Had Mike or Weston contacted Tye when they were looking into the deposit he'd made into Jack's account? Had they then told him about finding the ring as well? It was entirely possible. It was also possible that Tye had then called Edmond to prepare him exactly for the interview. Olivia felt uneasy.

"Had any of Tye's clients down here met Amanda?" Olivia continued.

"How would I know that?" said Edmond. "And why?"

"I was wondering if Tye ever brought his wife down here with him." If he hadn't that definitely struck Olivia as odd.

"I have no idea about that, really." Edmond became ill at ease once again. "I know he came down for business. Beyond that, he and I never shared all the details of his personal life."

"But you shared clientele, didn't you? Isn't it normal for people to talk about each other?" Olivia wanted more.

"I'm sure it is," said Edmond. "But no one ever mentioned Tye's wife to me. Why in the world should they?"

"Just wondering," said Olivia. "After all, everyone is talking about her now."

"Now it's entirely different," said Edmond. "She's all over the news."

"So you know nothing about Tye's marriage? Nobody ever commented that it was strange that he came here on his own so much?" Olivia tried just one last time.

"I'm beginning to resent this line of questioning." Edmond bristled. "You're asking me to insinuate something and I refuse to. I simply sold the man a ring for his wife. I told you that he was delighted to purchase it for her, wanted to make her happy. That's all I know. That's all I can tell you."

Edmond stood up then and cleared his throat to indicate the interview was over.

Olivia stood up as well as Edmond swiftly turned and led the way out of his office, right out onto the street.

Before she knew what happened, Olivia was outside alone walking along the winding streets. On the surface the interview had gone well. Edmond corroborated everything Tye had told her. But beyond that, he was an odd duck, too buttoned up, not entirely believable. He'd seemed ill at ease and way too formal with her as well. There was no way Olivia could point to anything to declare him an unreliable witness though, or justify spending any more time questioning him. Basically, the meeting hadn't been useful. It was a waste of time and energy. Olivia felt disappointed. Perhaps she would get some new ideas during her dinner with Wayne. Olivia definitely looked forward to that.

CHAPTER SIXTEEN

Wayne was coming at six o'clock to pick up Olivia. That gave them about an hour and a half for dinner before she had to leave for the airport to return to Key Largo that night.

As soon as Olivia returned to her apartment, she showered and dressed in an aqua silk summer dress with short sleeves and a scoop neckline. After putting on open sandals, she brushed her hair until it shone and felt good when she looked into the mirror. A lovely, bright, alert young woman looked back at her.

The bell to her apartment rang at a few minutes before six and Olivia went to the door to welcome Wayne. She opened the door and there he was, looking fantastic, dressed in a blue summer shirt, linen slacks, and a light jacket.

"Right on time," said Olivia, "come on in."

"You look wonderful, Olivia." Wayne couldn't look away.

"Thanks, so do you. Do you like my place?" she asked.

Wayne walked in and looked around. "I do, very much," he said. "I'd love to sit down, but we have a reservation a few blocks away in just a few minutes."

"Of course," said Olivia, "let's be on our way."

Olivia was surprised at how relaxing and reassuring it was to be with Wayne. It seemed as though they'd known each other forever. Probably because he'd helped her so much during such a difficult time, she guessed.

They left the apartment and walked a few blocks to the restaurant, chatting lightly about this and that. The restaurant was one that Olivia had been to before and loved. Along with the large windows, it had outdoor seating and plants everywhere.

Olivia and Wayne were seated and after ordering a light dinner, they looked at each other over a glass of red wine.

"This is an incredible first case you're working on," Wayne started.

"It's my third case, really." Olivia smiled.

"I mean it's your first case as a licensed PI," he added.

"You're right, it is incredible," Olivia agreed, "especially as I'm the only one convinced that Amanda could still be alive."

Wayne paused for a long moment. "Why are you convinced of that?"

"No reason in particular," Olivia murmured, "a gut instinct, maybe? You always told me to trust my gut instincts."

Wayne smiled. "Yes, and I stand by it. I guess I've said lots of things."

"And they've impacted me," said Olivia.

Wayne put his glass of wine down. "I'm glad of that," he replied softly. "You've impacted me as well."

Olivia finished what was left in her glass.

"And it looks like you're doing beautifully in general," Wayne continued. "Seems like you're getting over Todd and moving on."

Olivia brushed her hair back from her face lightly. "I'm getting over Todd more and more," she agreed. Olivia wasn't sure what Wayne meant by moving on, though. As the warm breezes blew in upon them, she wondered if Wayne was asking if she was dating again.

"What do you mean by moving on?" Olivia finally asked.

"Well, for starters, you've changed your profession, and the city you live in," Wayne elaborated. "You're working for yourself now, which in and of itself is amazing And, you're on a spectacular, high-profile case."

Olivia nodded. Wayne hadn't mentioned a thing about dating. All the changes he mentioned had seemed natural to her, almost inevitable. Olivia wanted to ask Wayne what else he meant by moving on. But fortunately the waiter came over with dinner at that moment and she thought better of it.

Both Olivia and Wayne were hungry and they dove into their food quickly.

"What's the main theory about the case now?" Wayne asked as he ate.

"The police haven't stated one officially yet," Olivia replied. "I believe they feel the wildlife got her, though."

"Do you believe that as well?" asked Wayne.

"No," Olivia replied emphatically. "Right now, for me, the husband's a definite suspect. Amanda's friend Irma said there were really rough spots in their marriage. And now, finally, Tye's confirmed it as well."

"I'd say there are rough spots in every marriage, wouldn't you?" Wayne looked at Olivia searchingly.

"Sure," Olivia answered, "just depends how rough, and how long they last."

"Good answer." Wayne liked that.

"Tye wired money into Jack's account and bought that diamond ring." Olivia enumerated all that bothered her. "The jeweler, Edmond, practically echoed every word Tye said. He sounded totally rehearsed to me."

"Trust what you feel," Wayne responded quickly.

"Weston says just the opposite," Olivia couldn't help but say. "He's a meat and potatoes kind of guy. He's skeptical of speculation of any kind. Shuts it right down. He sticks to the facts almost blindly."

"I know lots of guys like that," Wayne commented. "Don't let him take you down."

"He doesn't." Olivia flipped her hair back off her shoulders. "He can get irritating, but that's about it."

"What do you really think happened to Amanda?" Wayne asked point-blank.

"I think Tye could have a girlfriend in the Keys," Olivia mused. "It's possible the ring was for her and he was waiting to give it to her after Amanda went missing."

"That's quite a theory." Wayne was taken aback.

"I was thinking that it was even possible that Tye's girlfriend could have had a hand in Amanda's disappearance," Olivia went on.

Wayne listened deeply and carefully. "You've got to be careful about going out too far on a limb without evidence," he suggested.

"I know I do," said Olivia.

"What other ideas are being floated around?" asked Wayne. "Did the police check into any pervs floating around in the area?"

"They didn't mention that much, really," Olivia replied. "It came up once briefly and the cops tossed it off. They said it was very unlikely, due to where she went missing."

"They're probably right," Wayne couldn't help but agree.

"What do you think happened, Wayne?" Olivia deeply wanted to hear his thoughts. "There's rumblings of the case going cold, being closed down."

"That's not good." Wayne didn't like it. "Keep searching for small details, little objects Amanda may have left behind. Talk more and more to the people she knew. There's something that happened in her life that could tell you the whole story. Someone knows something they're not letting on."

"How do you know?"

"It's always like that," Wayne replied quickly. "Cases like these are rotten for cops. No matter how hard they work nothing surfaces. It makes them look bad. Police always want to close cases like these down quickly. Don't let them."

Olivia was thrilled talking to Wayne. She felt more like herself again, uplifted.

"Thanks so much for validating what I was feeling," she murmured. "I needed that."

"Of course you did," said Wayne, finishing up what was left of his dinner.

"How's your work going, Wayne?" Olivia asked then.

"It's getting rougher for me on the force," Wayne said somberly, surprising Olivia. "I've become more and more involved in restorative justice."

"The Innocence Project?" Olivia asked.

"Yes, that and more," Wayne answered. "It's incredibly complicated and wonderful. Really fills the bill for me."

"How wonderful that you've found that." Olivia was delighted.

"Wonderful to you, maybe, but needless to say I'm catching a lot of blowback from the authorities. It's a different mindset from where I work."

"I realize," said Olivia, fascinated.

"Actually, more and more these days I've been thinking of going out on my own," Wayne added. "I'm so impressed with what you're doing."

Olivia was moved. "That would be wonderful, Wayne, really wonderful."

Wayne looked at her appreciatively. "Nice to hear someone's in my corner," he added.

"There's nothing like following your own truth," Olivia continued.

"That's what I tell myself day after day," said Wayne. "Since I was little all I cared about was justice."

"I remember, you told me," Olivia replied.

"You remember that?" Wayne was surprised.

"Yes, I do," said Olivia, "and it's beautiful."

"Well, thanks so much," said Wayne. "Now you've inspired me."

"How are you thinking of going out on your own?" asked Olivia.

"That's another question." Wayne looked up at her. "I'll tell you about it when we have more time."

Olivia was reminded suddenly that their time together tonight had to be brief. She had to leave for the airport in a short while and catch a plane up to Key Largo. For a quick moment she felt upset about it. She wanted to stay here in this wonderful café, eating a long, slow dinner with Wayne, hearing all he had to say. She felt short-changed.

"So sorry I have to run away so quickly," she said.

"I'm sorry too." Wayne put his fork down. "But work is calling. We'll have other opportunities."

They finished up quickly and Wayne insisted upon accompanying Olivia to the airport.

"It's not necessary," she said again and again.

"But I want to," he replied plainly, as they jumped into a cab and went on their way.

"Thanks for joining me," Olivia said as the cab slipped onto the main highway.

"Actually, it's the best place I can think of being right now," Wayne replied. "I love watching planes come and go in the evening. They remind me of big birds dipping into and out of the sky."

Olivia smiled. Wayne still had the same charm and ease of manner about him that had meant so much to her when Todd had been killed. She hadn't been able to focus much on Wayne then, but it was different now. Riding in the cab together, with nothing else between them, Olivia had a surprising and beautiful deep sense of peace.

*

The flight back was difficult. Olivia hadn't been ready to leave when she did. She was intrigued by Wayne and what he was thinking of and planning. As the plane dipped and rocked in the turbulent air, Olivia couldn't help remember her time in the Keys with Todd as well. It seemed as if one unexpected wave after another hit her down here.

Her phone rang suddenly then and Olivia picked up quickly, not knowing what was coming next. To Olivia's surprise, Amanda's friend Dale was on the other end, talking in a heated tone.

"They're talking about closing the case," Dale started, agitated. "I even heard it on the news. We can't let that happen. I have more information and I've got to tell you right away."

Olivia shivered. "What is it?"

"I want to tell you in person," Dale insisted. "I'll meet your plane at the airport and we can talk there."

"Why didn't you tell me before?" asked Olivia immediately.

"I couldn't tell you this before. Amanda said to keep it secret," Dale breathed. "But I have to now. We have to stop them from closing the case!"

"Yes, we do," Olivia agreed.

"So, I'll be there when the plane lands," Dale repeated. "Wait for me."

CHAPTER SEVENTEEN

The moment Olivia got off the plane she saw Dale there, waving at her. Her hair was blowing wildly in the evening air and she looked agitated. Dale ran over to Olivia immediately and pulled on her arm.

"Do you have to go to baggage claim?" she asked.

"No, I just have an overnight suitcase," said Olivia.

"Good," said Dale, pulling harder, "then come with me."

"Where are we going?" Olivia felt somewhat alarmed.

"We'll go to the bar at the airport and get a drink," said Dale. "Nobody will realize what we're doing there."

"What are we doing?" Olivia felt confused.

"I'm telling you something I never thought I would," Dale insisted. "I swore to Amanda I wouldn't tell a soul, ever. Swore it!"

"Okay, let's go." Olivia wanted to get there as fast as possible and hear what was on Dale's mind.

"If you ever find Amanda alive, you have to promise that you'll never tell her what I told you," Dale breathed as they rushed through the airport to the bar.

"Let's just focus on finding Amanda alive," said Olivia.

"No, you have to promise! I really mean it." Dale stopped short.

"Okay, I promise," said Olivia to Dale's great relief.

*

The bar was mostly empty when Olivia and Dale rushed in. Fortunately, there was an empty table in the corner and the two of them slipped in. Dale seemed extremely anxious, was perspiring profusely, but seemed determined at the same time.

"Okay, what's on your mind?" Olivia didn't want to waste any more time.

"Nobody knows this," Dale finally started, but then stopped cold. "I can't say it!"

"You have to," Olivia demanded.

"Amanda was pregnant," Dale finally breathed.

"Pregnant?" Olivia wasn't sure she was hearing correctly.

"Yes, three months pregnant and no one knew it! Except Irma and me."

"You're positive?" Olivia was stunned.

"I'm positive," Dale continued.

"Why didn't she tell Tye about it?"

"She just couldn't. There was no way," Dale replied.

"Why not?" Olivia was electrified. This was certainly startling news not only about Amanda, but about her relationship with Tye. "And why didn't Irma mention it to me? This is big news. It's important."

"Amanda swore both Irma and I to secrecy," Dale repeated nervously.

At that moment, both Olivia and Dale looked up and saw Irma walking toward them, distressed.

"What's Irma doing here?" Olivia was surprised.

"I told Irma I was going to tell you about the baby," Dale breathed. "I have to, there's no choice about it. I had no idea Irma decided to come as well."

"I'm sorry I'm late," Irma said the second she got to the table. "I was looking for both of you in the lounge instead."

"What are you doing here?" asked Dale immediately.

"This is too big for you to do alone," Irma breathed. "And I need to hear for myself everything Olivia says when she finds out."

"Okay, come sit down with us then," Dale responded, seeming relieved to have her friend close by.

As Irma went to get a chair and bring it to the table, Olivia looked around. A few more passengers were now seated at the bar, and through the windows she could see planes in the background, landing and taking off.

"Did you tell Olivia yet?" Irma asked the moment she was seated.

"Yes, I did," said Dale.

Olivia decided to pick up the conversation where she and Dale had left off.

"I asked Dale if Amanda had told Tye about the pregnancy," said Olivia, point-blank.

Irma's eyes opened wide. "No, of course not. Amanda couldn't tell him. How could she? She was having an affair with someone else." Irma's words dropped like a bomb on Olivia.

"An affair? You're sure?" Olivia couldn't catch her breath.

"Positive," Irma continued. "And besides that, Tye was away for almost the whole month when Amanda conceived."

"Wait a minute, slow down." Olivia was suddenly beside herself. Too much information was coming at her all at once. "You're telling me that not only was Amanda pregnant, but that Tye isn't the father of her child?"

"Exactly right." Irma took over. "Amanda and Tye definitely hadn't slept together for that whole month. And not much before that, either."

"What do you mean, not much?" Olivia was appalled.

"Tye wasn't that interested in her," Irma shot back.

"How do you know this?" Olivia felt the case coming unglued.

"Friends speak, they share their pain," Irma replied. "It was awful for Amanda that her own husband barely touched her. So she took a lover, someone completely different from Tye."

Olivia closed her eyes and then opened them abruptly. "And was Tye involved with someone else, too?" she asked.

"I wondered that myself," said Irma. "I even mentioned it to Amanda several times. But Amanda doubted it. He was just cold, through and through, she told me. But Amanda was also definitely scared though that Tye might realize she was pregnant."

"How could he possibly know?" asked Olivia.

"Amanda started throwing up a lot, right from the start of the pregnancy," Irma explained.

"I told Amanda that Tye would never put two and two together," Dale burst in then. "I kept trying to reassure her, but she had a funny feeling that he also knew about her and Randy."

"Randy? Was he the guy she was sleeping with?" asked Olivia.

"Right," said Dale.

"Who is he, anyway? Part of their inner circle of friends?"

"No, Randy's someone Amanda met working out at the gym," Irma interrupted. "He's no one special, just a drifter. He goes from town to town, works a job for a couple of years, then moves on. I told her their relationship would never amount to anything."

"Maybe that was all she wanted. Just a fling," said Dale.

"Was she in love with Randy?" Olivia breathed.

Dale shook her head vigorously. "Not at all," she replied. "The idea of being in love with Randy never entered Amanda's mind. She was in love with Tye if you asked me."

"But Tye wasn't in love with her," Irma broke in. "The harder Amanda tried, the more he pulled away."

"Sounds awful." Olivia was filled with sadness.

"It was awful, it is awful," Dale cried out. "Amanda deserved far better than that."

"Did Amanda sleep with Randy to get back at Tye?" Olivia's head started spinning. "Was she doing it out of vengeance?"

"I thought that myself," Dale whispered. "I said to her, Amanda, vengeance won't get you anywhere."

"It wasn't vengeance." Irma defended her friend intensely. "She did it because she was lonely. Amanda was very, very lonely."

"She wasn't planning to keep the baby, was she?" Olivia suddenly felt heartbroken for all of them.

"Of course she was," Irma replied. "Amanda said over and over there was no way anyone was taking the baby from her."

This turned everything upside down. "Then Amanda definitely didn't go out into the swamp with the idea of committing suicide, did she?" asked Olivia.

"Suicide? Never, ever," Dale breathed. "She was excited to have the baby. She said it was someone who would love her, finally."

"She was also terrified about having it," Irma broke in. "Amanda had no idea how to tell Tye, or what his reaction would be."

"Not a very good reaction, I imagine," said Olivia.

"But Amanda must have told him about the baby though, on this trip."

"No, she didn't," Irma strongly objected. "I was in touch with her every day and she told me she hadn't said a word about it."

"Did Amanda tell you every detail of her personal life?" asked Olivia, startled.

"Yes, everything," Irma smiled.

"That's one of the reasons Tye pulled away from her," Dale joined in. "Amanda's relationship with Irma bothered him. It got in the way."

"Let it bother him all he likes." Irma gritted her teeth. "It bothers me more that Amanda's gone missing, and for all we know by now, she's dead."

The three of them stopped cold and grew silent at the idea that Amanda's life was over. Olivia tried to grasp the horror Amanda must have gone through.

"Her pregnancy has to be connected to her going missing," Olivia breathed.

"It has to," said Dale. "I think so too."

"Maybe yes and maybe no?" Irma wasn't sure. "I'm going to give you Randy's contact information, Olivia. Talk to him and see what you think."

"He's down here too?" Olivia was astonished. If Randy was in the vicinity, there was no question but that he was a suspect as well.

"He wasn't down here when Amanda went missing," Dale replied, "but he's come recently to join a search team."

"Was Randy in love with Amanda?" asked Olivia. "Was he hoping she'd leave Tye and be with him?"

"I always thought so," Dale whispered, "but Amanda didn't."

"It doesn't matter what Randy was or wasn't feeling." Irma's voice grew sharp as a sword. "Just go talk to him right away and see what he has to say."

"Is there anything else at all you have to tell me?" Olivia asked before getting up.

Irma scrawled Randy's contact information on a napkin as Dale began to cry softly.

"Call Randy immediately," Irma repeated. "He's staying with a search team three miles away. Then, you must tell us everything he said."

Olivia took the napkin with Randy's information as Dale and Irma both got up suddenly, and without another word, rushed away together, arm in arm.

Olivia sat at the table another few minutes, turning the napkin over and over in her hand. As she did Amanda's life sprawled out before her suddenly, a tapestry of deceit, loneliness, and fear.

Olivia left the bar then and on her way back to the hotel put in a call to Randy. To her surprise he picked up the phone. Olivia asked him to come right over to her lobby. There was no time to be wasted at all.

To Olivia's delight, Randy agreed instantly. In fact, he seemed relieved that Olivia contacted him and wanted to talk.

*

"I loved her, adored her, she was the whole world to me," Randy insisted the second he and Olivia were seated alone out of sight or hearing, in the back of the hotel.

"She was a married woman," Olivia responded.

"That was no marriage at all, it was worth nothing," Randy barked. "Besides, in the beginning she came on to me."

Randy was tall and toned with dark hair, large muscles, and a scar on the bottom of his face. Rough and tumble, he looked ready for anything.

"You're telling me that Amanda flirted with you and approached you?" Olivia asked with as much equilibrium as she could muster.

"She certainly did. If you ask the gym rats around, they all saw it," Randy proclaimed. "The guys all talked about how I got lucky. I did nothing wrong at all. A fella's got a right to go after happiness."

"Everyone has that right," Olivia agreed.

"Including Amanda," Randy emphasized as his jaw protruded. "She had a right to be happy, didn't she?"

"She found happiness with you?" asked Olivia.

"Oh boy, did she ever." Randy smirked.

"Did Amanda tell you she was leaving her husband for you?" Olivia wanted the whole story, every gory detail.

Randy laughed. "She didn't have to tell me anything," he proclaimed. "She'd have left him in a second if I would have had her."

Olivia was totally repelled. "What do you mean if you would have had her?"

"We got on, if you know what I mean," Randy said.

"No, I don't," said Olivia.

"We did real good together," Randy elaborated.

"In bed?" Olivia felt disconsolate.

"That's right, you got it." He grinned.

"Not so funny now, is it?" snapped Olivia. "She's gone."

"Gone but not forgotten," crooned Randy.

What in the world was he thinking? Olivia couldn't imagine what Amanda ever saw in this kind of man. Why would she choose him? Olivia decided to jump in whole hog and find out all she could.

"Did you know Amanda was pregnant?" Olivia asked pointedly.

"What are you talking about?" Randy's forehead creased.

"Amanda was expecting a baby." Olivia made it more explicit.

"Come on, you got to be nuts!" Randy replied.

"Most likely she was carrying your baby, Randy." Olivia wasn't holding back.

"My baby?" Randy looked as though someone had shot him in the gut. "That's impossible."

"Why?" asked Olivia.

"Because she never said a word about it to me," he muttered, "and believe me, she talked a blue streak about everything."

"The DNA testing will give us the final word," Olivia replied.

"Carrying my baby?" Randy was trying to get his mind around it.

"Are you ready for that?" Olivia wasn't letting up. "Want to be a father?"

"Hell, no," he shot back. "Actually, I never thought about it."

"Well, you better start thinking about it now," Olivia replied.

"Why should I?" Randy became combative.

"Because when we find her, that's what you're gonna be," said Olivia. "The father of a baby."

Randy shook his head back and forth in bewilderment. "But what are the chances you're gonna find her?" he finally muttered. "Less than one percent, they say."

"We're gonna find her, Randy," Olivia insisted.

"Well, if you find her, she's got a husband and so the baby is his," Randy muttered.

Olivia took a long, painful breath.

"You think her disappearance has something to do with the baby?" Randy became incredulous.

"It certainly could," Olivia answered. "Women are killed for lesser mistakes than that."

CHAPTER EIGHTEEN

After Randy left it was absolutely clear that Olivia had to speak with Tye again. Did he know that Amanda was pregnant? It was certainly a possibility. Did Tye think she was having his baby? These questions, right now, were at the crux of the entire case. All the answers to Amanda's disappearance could hinge on this.

Early the next morning, even before she had breakfast, Olivia put a call in to Tye. Thankfully he was still in his room.

"Don't go anywhere for the next hour," she told him. "I have to come right over and talk to you. Go downstairs and meet me in the lobby."

"Why?" asked Tye, alarmed. "More news?"

"Yes," said Olivia grimly. "I'll be there in a little while and we'll talk."

Olivia grabbed a quick cup of coffee and a bite of the muffin that was in her room. Then she dressed in a short, paisley summer dress and made her way directly to Tye's hotel. As instructed, he was in the lobby waiting for her.

"I don't know how much more I can take of this," was the first thing Tye said as Olivia walked over to him.

"Let's go to the back garden and talk," Olivia replied.

Tye nodded and the two of them made their way to the back, walking underneath winding vines, along a narrow cobblestone path.

"Okay, tell me!" said Tye as they found narrow chairs to sit on.

Olivia had to broach all of this slowly, carefully ease into the truth.

"Tye," Olivia started, "was Amanda well when she came on this trip?"

"What do you mean well?" Tye shivered. "Do you mean was she upset, depressed, nervous?"

"Was she?"

"Not at all. I told you that before," he retorted. "She was very excited to be here."

"I meant was Amanda physically well?" Olivia continued. "Was anything going on with her physical condition?"

"Nothing at all." Tye looked at Amanda oddly. "She was same as always, strong and active. She was stronger than me, in her own way. I was the one who got sick that morning, remember?"

"Yes, I do remember," said Olivia, wondering how to get at it. "Had Amanda gained any weight recently?"

"What are you talking about?" Tye looked momentarily confused.

"Was there a change in her physical condition?" Olivia proceeded cautiously.

"Not that I know of," said Tye slowly. "What are you trying to get at?"

"Did you know that Amanda was pregnant?" Olivia finally blurted out.

A wave of shock and silence filled the early morning air as Olivia spoke.

"Pregnant?" Tye finally uttered, in disbelief. "What in hell are you talking about? It's impossible."

"Nothing is impossible, is it?" Olivia murmured.

"Yes, this is!" Tye seemed absolutely certain.

"Why?" Olivia looked at him plainly.

"Just take my word for it." Tye grew flustered. "Who the hell told you this crazy news?"

Despite her promises, Olivia had to tell him. She needed to shake the full truth loose from him, the way you shake old leaves off rotten branches.

"Irma and Dale told me!" said Olivia.

At that Tye jumped up and paced back and forth. "Sure, I could believe Irma would say something like that. That lousy friend of hers would make up anything to make me look like a jerk! But how can you go along with it? Do you think Irma would know something so personal about Amanda and I wouldn't?"

"Anything is possible," Olivia repeated.

"I hate Irma and you should too!" Tye's voice grew louder. "She doesn't mean well by Amanda and she doesn't mean well by me. She never did. I told you."

"Tye." Olivia got up and stood beside him. "Irma also said that Amanda was three months pregnant!"

Tye looked far too upset now for Olivia to add that someone else was the father. Tye looked away, far into the distance.

"Three months pregnant? Do you really think Amanda could keep this from me for three months?" Then he grew quiet and thought it over. "No, it's impossible she'd be three months pregnant anyway. I was gone that entire month that she would have conceived. So, it's all nonsense. And a convenient story! There's no way anyone can check it without access to Amanda's body. So they can say anything they want, can't they? It's all garbage."

Tye had a point. There certainly was an off chance that both Irma and Dale were lying. But why would they? What would they have to gain?

Tye rubbed his heel into the ground. "Look, I had enough of you for now." He had a disgusted look on his face. "This is the best you can come up with? Fantasies and lies?"

He turned swiftly then and without another word, ran back down the cobblestone path to the hotel completely alone. Olivia stood there looking after him. He had a right to be as upset as he was. This was intense, troubling information. She wondered if she should have shared it with him without corroboration. But Olivia wanted to see his response. If Tye knew it was true he might have said something that could have led Olivia to Amanda.

After Tye was well out of sight, Olivia began walking back down the trail. She had to go to the police station now and report all this information to them, no matter how farfetched it seemed.

*

It was especially hot and humid today and on her way to the station Olivia began perspiring. Was it possible that Tye was right and Irma and Dale had made this all up? If so, they had a hidden agenda, might even be suspects themselves. Olivia thought about bringing up that possibility with Mike and Weston.

When she arrived at the station, to Olivia's surprise it was busier than she'd expected. People were coming and going all over the place. Had the investigation into Lilly Feld taken hold? Most had heard much about the woman's whose remains had been found in the gator's mouth. It was grisly news and had now caused a commotion. Once again Olivia wondered if there could be any connection between Lilly and Amanda. How could it be a coincidence that they both went missing in the same spot?

Olivia arrived at Mike's office, which was open. Without knocking, she walked right in. Both Mike and Weston were seated at the main table riffling through papers. They looked up when Olivia entered, surprised.

"What are you doing here?" asked Mike.

Olivia was relieved to see both of them. "More news," she announced.

"Great." Weston stood up. "Come on in. You're lucky you found us here. It's usually better to call first."

"Just taking my chances," Olivia said, sitting down.

"What's the news, Olivia?" asked Mike.

"I can wait until you're finished going over these papers," Olivia offered.

"No, we're actually done," Mike replied. "We've been investigating Jack Healey and the bonus he received from Tye. We talked to Jack about it already, and it seems his nephew Frank, the other guide, got some of the money, too. Frank's coming in to see us in a little while. This is actually a perfect time for you to tell us what else you found."

"What did Jack tell you about the bonus?" Olivia was fascinated.

"He said it's normal for people to send extra gratuities for special attention on the tours. Jack gave part of the money to Frank, who was the guide that particular day."

"Are you going to check and see if it really is normal for people to send gratuities?" asked Olivia.

"There's a limit to what we have time to check out, Olivia," Weston interrupted. "We've got to throw away the pebbles and look for gold."

"Anyway, what's your news?" Mike interrupted.

Olivia got right to the heart of the matter. "Amanda's friends Irma and Dale told me that Amanda was pregnant."

Mike and Weston stopped in their tracks.

"Amanda's friends also said that her baby did not belong to Tye."

Both Mike and Weston grew stony and silent. "Whoa, this is something else," Weston finally muttered.

"The baby didn't belong to Tye?" Mike was scratching his face. "In other words, you're tell me that Amanda was cheating on him?"

"The man she was having an affair with, Randy, happens to be in Key Largo now," Olivia added. "He came down a little while ago to join the search."

"This is big news." Mike now looked askance.

"It's fantastic news!" said Weston.

Bolstered, Olivia continued. "I've actually spoken to Randy already and he has an airtight alibi for when Amanda disappeared. He was back home in Connecticut working. Lots of people saw him there."

"That has to be checked out, of course," Weston muttered.

"It will be," said Mike. "It's easy to confirm. Mike then turned to Olivia. "Does Tye know about all of this?"

"I spoke to Tye as well just now," Olivia added.

"What are you? A flash of lightning?" Weston quipped.

"Just doing my job," Olivia answered plainly. "Tye claims to know nothing of Amanda's pregnancy. He seemed shaken to the bone when I told him. So I didn't tell him the baby wasn't his, yet. Tye believes Amanda's friends made up the story."

"Why would they?" Weston looked confused.

"Why not?" asked Mike. "They could hate Tye for some reason and want to make him look guilty as hell."

"Yeah," Weston agreed. "If Amanda was pregnant, especially with someone else's child, Tye would become a prime suspect. But even if the baby was his, you know how many husbands kill their pregnant wives? Pregnancy can bring out the worst in a guy, and there's no way of predicting it."

Olivia felt a long, slow chill.

"I remember when my ex-wife suddenly got pregnant, I couldn't sleep for nights," Weston went on. "The thought of being a father was overwhelming. I kept thinking the kid would get between us, take my wife's time and energy away."

That was a horrible way to feel and Olivia felt disturbed hearing it. It was also upsetting to hear that many men felt this way.

"How did you feel after your ex-wife had the baby?" she asked, tentatively.

"She had a miscarriage the second month," Weston replied. "It happened naturally, by itself. At that time I remember thinking it was best for us all."

Weston's story deeply saddened Olivia. It was every woman's worst nightmare to have her husband feel that way.

"So, what's the next step here?" Mike became agitated.

"We need evidence that corroborates the pregnancy," Weston said. "Would Amanda's friends have it?"

"I believe Irma and Amanda spoke every day," Olivia replied. "You could get their phone records."

"Good idea," said Mike. "If we can confirm the pregnancy, we then also need evidence about whether or not Tye knew. If he knew about it, then he lied to us."

"We might be able to get that from the phone records as well," Weston mused. "I'll get on it right after we're done talking to Frank."

"What's Frank coming in again for?" Olivia wanted to be thoroughly informed.

"We need to talk to Frank about his part of the bonus," Mike informed her. "We've got to make sure he really received it, and that he backs Jack's story up about what the money was for."

The police were being thorough and Olivia respected that.

"You can stay here and join in when Frank arrives," Mike added. "He'll be here in a few minutes."

"I'd like that," said Olivia, pleased to be included.

*

Frank arrived in about ten minutes, looking weather-beaten, messy, and disgruntled.

"Sit down, Frank," said Weston, as soon as he entered the room. "This will only take a few minutes."

"Good," said Frank, "because a few minutes is all I got. What did I do now?"

"How much of a bonus did Jack give you for Amanda's tour?" Mike jumped right in.

"What the hell are you talking about?" Frank seemed blindsided.

"Did you get a bonus at all for working that tour?" Weston added.

Frank tapped his fingers on the table. "Yeah, that's right. I remember, Jack gave me a few extra bucks for doing the job. He said to take extra good care of Amanda, let her do whatever she wanted." Frank looked up at them warily. "Is that what this is still about?"

"Still?" said Mike. "We haven't found Amanda yet."

"I got it," Frank burst out. "You're still looking to pin her death on someone."

"I wouldn't say we're trying to pin it on anyone," Weston broke in. "We're still searching for clues as to what exactly happened."

"You don't need to keep searching for clues." Frank became irritated. "It was pretty simple. She got off in the swamps where she shouldn't have, and something lousy happened. Nobody knows what. Nobody was there with her. I didn't get off the boat with her and neither did my uncle Jack."

"No, you didn't, that's true," Mike added. "But someone still could have set her up for a hit."

Frank's face soured. "There are easier ways to do that." He scowled. "Who the hell's going to go into a dangerous part of the glades to take her down?"

"Why not? It's a perfect setup," said Mike. "It makes it look like it was a natural disaster."

Frank paused, had to agree, "Like what happened to Lilly Feld?" he murmured. "Now, that's a natural disaster if I ever saw one."

"Yes, it was," Weston mumbled.

"But no one's making such a big fuss about Lilly, are they?" Frank started to stew. "Who was she anyway? A lost girl, probably a runaway. I see lots of them wandering around down here. No one cares a bit about them, but I do whatever I can to help."

Olivia was startled to learn that. "What do you do, Frank?"

"Try to warn these girls of danger, steer them off the streets and back into their rotten lives," he muttered. "No matter how rotten it is, I tell them, it's better than being trapped or dead."

Olivia was touched to hear this.

"Lilly Feld went missing from her home in Kentucky a few months before she died," Frank went on. "No one even reported it. She came down here and was out on the streets. And you see what happened next."

"Frank's right," Mike had to agree. "It's hard to keep track of them all."

"So, how exactly did she end up in the mouth of an alligator?" Olivia was horrified.

"Who knows?" Frank shrugged. "I'd say someone caught her, had fun, and killed her somewhere else. Then they came down here to toss the body."

"Who?" Olivia called out. "Who?"

"Calm down, Olivia, calm down," said Mike.

"This deserves to be thoroughly investigated," Olivia insisted.

"Lots of things deserve to be thoroughly investigated," Mike barked back.

"Hell, there's that halfway house for sex predators not so far away," Frank barked, too.

"What halfway house?" Olivia was stunned.

"It's not close by, it's fifty miles away." Weston joined the fray. "And Lilly Feld made herself an open target. Amanda did not."

"Enough, enough." Mike stood up. "We're not here about Lilly Feld. It's Amanda we're focusing on now."

"Okay, so I told you again what happened to her." Frank calmed down a little. "And what's the big deal about my uncle getting a bonus from Tye? Jack's a good man! Don't set him up for trouble because you don't have anyone else!"

At that Frank stood up briskly. "I'm finished here now. Told you all I know."

Weston stood up as well. "It's fine for now, Frank, you can go."

"For now? I'm not coming back again, either," Clearly Frank had had enough of it all. He flew out of the room quickly.

Mike and Weston looked at each other and shook their heads as he left.

"We've got nothing to hold him on," Mike said to Weston. "There's nothing illegal about getting a bonus."

"Not illegal," Weston agreed, "but it raises questions about Tye and Jack. For all we know, the person who wrote that note about Jack was really onto something."

"Are you closer to finding out who wrote it?" Olivia asked.

"No, we're not," said Weston, sullenly. "The fingerprints don't match anything in the records, and the DNA doesn't either. So your information is a good next step. We'll check out the phone records of Irma's conversations with Amanda. See if she was really pregnant and if Tye knew about it or not."

Olivia was delighted that she'd brought this information to them. "I'd also like a warrant to get into Tye's room and check it again for myself," she said. "Hopefully there's some evidence planted there that he knew about the baby, too."

"Unlikely," said Weston.

"No, it's a good idea," Mike agreed quickly. "I'll get you the warrant right away, Olivia, and you go check Tye's room."

"So, go if you have to." Weston backed down. "Tye's usually out of the hotel in the evenings, at that club with his friends. That's the best time to go in and take a look."

*

Olivia went back to her hotel room to wait for the warrant and the all clear to search Tye's room again. As she lay down on her couch resting, her phone rang. Probably Mike or Weston, she thought, picking up.

"Hope you didn't forget about me already." Wayne was on the other end.

Olivia smiled. His call was unexpected and welcome. "How could I forget our wonderful dinner?" she said.

"Glad to hear that," said Wayne lightly. "Rumor is again that your case might be closing down soon. True?"

"Don't believe those rumors." Olivia laughed. "Actually, just the opposite is true. Things are heating up again. There have been interesting developments since I saw you."

"What?" asked Wayne.

"There's a chance that Amanda's pregnant," Olivia whispered into the phone. "And that it's not Tye's child."

"My God." Wayne sounded startled. "That's huge."

"We're holding it close to the vest," said Olivia. "Right now in the process of corroborating the news."

"Good for you," said Wayne, engaged. "If it's true, it doesn't look good for Tye."

"You've got that right," said Olivia.

"Be careful, Olivia." Wayne's voice lowered. "If it's foul play, you're standing right in the middle of it. You never know who'll they take down next."

"I know," said Olivia.

"Are the guys on the police force watching over you?" Wayne went on.

"They are, they're good," Olivia responded. "They're including me in everything."

"Fine," said Wayne, suddenly jittery. "But keep me in the loop, too, please. This is a tricky business."

"Of course I will," said Olivia, pleased that he cared so much.

CHAPTER NINETEEN

Amanda rallied as he slept, crumpled up in the corner, unaware of what was going. A bolt of electricity and heat had suddenly shot through her veins, stirring her from head to toe. As the sudden strength coursed through her, Amanda knew what it meant. Before you die a burst of energy can flood you, offering one last taste of life. Amanda trembled as the power enveloped her, spurring her on. It was demanding that she pull out of her downward spiral, the one that sent her falling into a world of dust.

The energy pushed Amanda to drag herself along the floor to the edge of the cabin. Every muscle ached and her heart beat heavily as she headed toward the small opening in the back. She had to do it silently too, so as not to wake him.

As she slithered along, Amanda feared any sound would jar him out of his slumber. He'd be up and all over her then, again. He was fanatic in his obsession to hold her there and watch her die slowly. Why? she wondered. Tell me, she'd begged him over and over. He refused to reply. Once, their eyes had met, but only once. When they did, his eyes were empty and blank.

Now, finally at the opening of the hut, Amanda paused. Could she do it? Was it possible? Was this strange power she'd suddenly been given a sign that she was destined to live? She pulled herself up slowly and rattled the door with her hands. It had to open just a little more before she could get through.

To her horror the door suddenly pushed against a post, making a loud crackling sound. It could wake him. He would kill her then. She couldn't let that stop her. Amanda pushed harder, forcing the door to open so she could slip through. Then a louder, fiercer sound burst out.

"What's that? What's that?" he grumbled, awakening.

Terrified, with all her strength, Amanda slid through the tiny opening, hoping to roll away, hide in the grass, anything she could think of.

For a precious second she was outside, free. She looked up at the crazy stars shining overhead and sucked in all the air she could breathe. Then she flinched as she heard his heavy footsteps closing in behind her.

"Save me, help me," Amanda managed to utter to the darkness, as she suddenly felt his thick, heavy hands on her shoulders, pulling her back into the blackness of the forlorn shack.

*

Olivia waited until nightfall to enter Tye's room again. As Weston had predicted, the room was empty. Tye wasn't there. Olivia walked in gingerly, feeling something inside was waiting for her.

Olivia immediately began opening Tye's bureau drawers, searching each one carefully and then closing them again. They were impeccably neat with nothing out of order. And there was nothing else to find inside.

Olivia then glanced at two suitcases standing in the corner of the room. She went over and inspected them carefully. One had Tye's name on the outside. The other belonged to Amanda. Most likely his suitcase would be empty, but you never knew.

Olivia opened Tye's suitcase immediately. The main part was empty, but there were other compartments, zipped tightly closed. Olivia began opening one after another. In one compartment were tissues, some business cards in another, and a small pen in yet another. When she opened the last compartment, though, a folded envelope was stashed inside. Olivia opened it quickly and unfolded a paper inside.

Olivia read the paper and gasped. Here it was! Lying right in the palm of her hand were the results of Amanda's pregnancy test. Positive! On the margins were calculations written in hand of exactly how far along the pregnancy had gone. Tye must have found the results, taken them, and hidden them away.

Olivia looked at the results of the test closely and shuddered. There was definitely no question. Tye knew that Amanda was pregnant. He also knew how far along she was. He had to have known then that the baby did not belong to him.

Tye had lied to them all. Repeatedly. Olivia's hands trembled as she slipped the evidence into her pocketbook and quickly made her way out of the hotel room.

Clutching her bag under her arm, Olivia slipped out of the hotel into the dark night and looked up at the sky. An unusually bright array of stars shone above her, as if guiding her along. Thrilled, sad, and shaken, Olivia walked slowly to her hotel a few blocks away. It was easy now to imagine that Tye had been complicit in Amanda's death. But there were still questions to be answered. How did he make it happen? And what was Jack's role? This was the evidence they all had been waiting for. Olivia had to call it in to the police immediately. There wasn't a moment to waste.

The moment Olivia returned to her room, she put a call in to Mike. As she expected, he answered immediately.

"I've got it," she breathed.

"Got what?" Mike sounded on edge.

"Tye knew all about Amanda's pregnancy," Olivia started. "He lied to us."

"Prove it." Mike didn't mince words.

"I found a copy of the results of her pregnancy test in his suitcase," Olivia breathed. "And on the margin of the edge was written how far along she was."

"My God." Mike was shaken.

"What are we going to do now?" Olivia was suddenly beside herself.

"Arrest Tye immediately," Mike proclaimed. "We'll bring him in tonight and you get to the station first thing in the morning for the interrogation."

*

Tye looked pale and shaken, sitting there huddled over in his seat in the police interrogation room. The morning light came in through a half-open window, and an overhead fan whirled the warm air around in the room.

Mike, Weston, Tommy, and a few others Olivia didn't know sat opposite Tye across a long table. Olivia sat between Mike and Weston, feeling scared.

"Okay, Tye, we have all the evidence we need here in front of us." Mike started the questioning.

Tye's eyebrows arched as if he were above it all, looking down at them in amusement.

"You're involved with your wife's death, it's obvious!" Mike wasn't pulling any punches.

"Ridiculous." Tye distanced himself further.

"Now just tell us what you did with the body," Mike went on methodically.

"Wait a minute." Tye bristled, "Last I heard Amanda is still missing. There's no body. You have no evidence at all that she is dead."

"Don't play games with me, Tye." Mike didn't like it.

"I'm just stating the simple facts," Tye shot back.

"But the simple facts aren't good enough any longer," Mike countered. "Whatever the hell you say means nothing. You lied to us all along, didn't you?"

"I told half truths." Tye was doing his best to try to wiggle out of it. It wasn't working though. There was no wiggle room left.

"You told us you didn't know that Amanda was pregnant, said that her friends were making the story all up. You said that, didn't you?" Mike was unrelenting.

"Yes, I did," Tye agreed.

"Why?" Weston burst into the conversation.

Tye felt better speaking to Weston and turned his whole attention to him. "Because it's nobody's damn business if Amanda was or wasn't pregnant," he said. "I was trying to save face."

"What guy has to save face because his wife is pregnant?" Tommy couldn't help but join in.

"It wasn't just that she was pregnant." Tye grew inflamed.

"It was that the baby didn't belong to you!" Mike was back on it. "That's what you had to save face from, isn't it?"

"Something like that." Tye became disturbed.

"Don't give me any more of your half truths." Mike was insistent. "We have notes written in your handwriting on the side of her pregnancy test that calculated just how far along she was."

Tye blanched.

"From those calculations you figured that the baby couldn't be yours. Right?" Mike continued.

"It was most unlikely that the baby was mine." Tye spoke in a bitter tone now.

"We heard you were traveling during the whole month that Amanda conceived," Mike added.

"You heard that from who?" Tye bristled again. "Irma?"

"It doesn't matter who." Mike seemed unwilling to tell him that it was Olivia who had brought them the information. "It's true, isn't it, though? You weren't around when Amanda conceived the baby."

"No, I wasn't." Tye stared at Mike fiercely. "So, now I'm being made a fool of for the entire world to see."

Weston shook his head slowly. "It happens to lots of us, Tye," he commented. "This isn't about being a fool."

"What is it about, then?" Tye spoke more heatedly.

"It's about finding Amanda." Olivia broke into the heated conversation.

"What's the connection between her cheating on me, and finding her body? I don't get it." said Tye.

"I didn't say finding her body, I said finding Amanda! Alive, hopefully," Olivia protested.

"Yeah, yeah," Tye muttered.

"Are you telling us then that she's definitely dead?" Olivia was all over it.

"I never said anything like that. You're twisting my words, every one of you!" snapped Tye.

"What the hell did you do with your wife?" Mike burst back in.

"What did *I* do with her?" Tye acted as if he couldn't believe what he was hearing. "You've got to be crazy or something. You're trying to blame her disappearance on me now?"

The tension in the room grew thicker as the fan overhead kept whirring.

"Convenient, isn't it?" Tye added. "You're taking a painful personal fact in my relationship and blowing it up to blame me for murder now!"

"Lots of guys have trouble when their wives get pregnant." Weston took over. "The statistics show it."

"So, I'm a statistic now?" said Tye.

"And on top of that, Amanda cheated on you." Mike rubbed it in.

"Don't use that word," Tye suddenly shouted, startling everyone.

"She slept with someone else." Weston tried another tack, slamming the reality into Tye's face.

"She cheated on you, cheated on you," Tommy kept repeating, obviously trying to get him to spill the whole truth out.

"Shut up." Tye turned straight on him.

"It happens to all of us, Tye," Weston was compelled to add, making it seem as if he had gone through this nightmare as well.

"I don't care who the hell it happens to," Tye burst out suddenly. "It doesn't happen to me!"

"And what do you do if it does?" Mike stood up.

"It doesn't happen to me," Tye repeated, outraged.

"But it did," Tommy burst out.

Mike had enough of these games. "If you don't tell us exactly what happened to Amanda, we're taking you in for obstruction of justice."

"You can't do that." Tye was beside himself.

"Yes, we can," Mike differed. "There's proof you knew Amanda was pregnant and that the baby belonged to someone else. That goes to motive. Plenty of it. Did you bring her down here to get revenge?"

"Of course he did. This is a case of vengeance, pure and simple." Tommy backed Mike up.

"Go to hell," Tye spit out, shaken to the core. "Okay, you're right. I knew about her pregnancy! And I knew the bitch was involved with someone else, too."

Olivia gasped. "The bitch?" she muttered, hurt to the core.

"Yeah, she was a bitch." Tye turned on his heel toward Olivia. "And don't defend her, whatever you do."

"I'm not defending her, but you told me you loved her," Olivia shot back. "You said you bought that ring for her to make peace!"

"I said that and I meant it." Tye was inflamed. "I did buy that ring to make peace. But then I thought better of it. I couldn't sleep all night after I found out about the baby. And that it didn't belong to me. All kinds of thoughts went through my head. First I thought she and I could get past this. Why not? Everyone makes mistakes, I thought."

"And the marriage wasn't perfect all along anyway, was it?" Olivia couldn't help add. "You spent a lot of time away from her, too, didn't you?"

"I did," Tye agreed. "Because I had to. She made me nuts. I did what I could to make her happy, but in return, she made me crazy."

"Hey, fella, it happens to all of us," Weston proclaimed.

"Not like this, she was a hard one to handle." Tye turned to Weston, gratefully.

"I can believe it, I can," said Weston.

"How was Amanda hard to handle?" Olivia wanted to keep the discussion on track.

Mike stood up, though, raised his hand and put a stop to all of it. "It doesn't matter how hard she was to handle, or what she did, you don't kill someone off because of that!"

"Who said I killed her off?" Tye was furious. "I bought her a new ring, didn't I? I paid Jack extra money to give her a terrific tour. I wanted to make things right!"

"But she disappeared then, didn't she?" Mike countered.

"That wasn't my fault," Tye suddenly wailed.

"Come on, man, don't tell me you didn't have a hand in it," Mike was like a bulldog, refusing to let go.

"Listen." Tye stepped a few feet closer to him. "You're right, I did think of killing her off. At times I wanted to. Who wouldn't? In fact, I actually planned to do it, believe it or not! I thought of ways I could help her fall into the swamp and stay down there forever."

The room grew stiff and silent as Tye's words invaded the day.

124

"But I didn't get the chance to. I didn't do this!" Tye insisted. "Someone else got to her before I did. I've been made a fool of two times now!"

The silence grew deeper.

"Who? Why?" asked Weston, obviously shaken as well.

"I don't know who, or why," Tye answered. "Maybe the guy she was sleeping with? Maybe he had enough of her too."

That didn't go over at all, though. "Randy's down here now," Olivia spoke up. "He came down to search for her. I had a chance to speak to him and he has an airtight alibi."

"You actually met the bastard?" Tye was suddenly incensed again.

"He wasn't in Key Largo when it happened. He had no reason to want her killed off," Olivia continued.

"And you have a reason," Tommy muttered.

"Yeah, I do," Tye agreed. "I have a very good reason to get her. But I also have a reason to make things right. I felt both ways at the same time."

"If you tell us exactly how you arranged for her to go missing and where she is now, things will go better for you," Mike said bluntly.

"I didn't do it," Tye insisted.

"We'll have to call Jack in again as well then, and see how well he knew you. What the hell did you really wire him that bonus for? To get her out further into the swamp, and then what?"

"You've got to believe me," Tye demanded. "I didn't do this. I planned to do something, but it never happened. It wasn't me. You've got to believe me."

"But we don't," answered Mike in a second flat.

"You can't prove a thing," Tye insisted.

"We've got motivation and opportunity," Mike answered. "The rest will fall into place in no time flat."

Tye's guilt seemed to be written all over him. The police had no choice but to lock him up. And Jack also had to be taken in to see how he fit into the picture. Case closed.

"We couldn't have done this without you, Olivia." Mike came over and extended his hand. "You've been a tremendous help. We looked into the phone calls, but there was nothing we could use for hard evidence."

Olivia shook hands with Mike tentatively. Something deep within didn't feel right. She had no idea what was bothering her, though.

"Great job." Weston came over and joined them as well.

"Thanks, Weston," Olivia replied.

"You don't look very happy about this," Weston went on.

"I'll be happy when we actually find Amanda," Olivia said. "Until then I still have questions."

"There are always questions." Weston's voice grew softer. "And I know how hard it is for you to let go. But don't hold your breath. You can't imagine how many missing people never turn up again."

CHAPTER TWENTY

The case was closed. She returned to her hotel, thinking it was time to pack and return to Key West. Olivia was uneasy about it, though. How could she leave before finding Amanda? It felt wrong to leave her here alone.

When Olivia got back to her hotel, the story had been blasted all over the news. ***Husband complicit in the disappearance of his wife. Case closed!*** The search was likely to be called off soon as well.

Olivia couldn't believe it. She felt as if they had barely begun. Her phone suddenly rang and she was afraid this could be an official thank-you and goodbye from the police. She certainly hoped it wasn't reporters calling for her input.

When Olivia picked up, it was Wayne.

"It's true this time? Case closed?" he asked. "It's over?"

Olivia was relieved to be talking to him. "They believe they've got enough on Tye to make it stick now," she replied.

"And what do you think?" Wayne countered, fast.

"I'm not at peace with this," Olivia breathed. "There's more here than meets the eye. There's no way I'm ready to let go."

"Trust your gut," Wayne whispered hoarsely.

"How can we stop searching when there's no sign at all of Amanda?" she went on. "Weston said lots of missing persons are never seen or heard from again, though."

"That's true," Wayne added, "but trust your gut anyway."

Olivia liked his response, appreciated it.

"What's your take on what happened?" Wayne pressed further.

"I've been thinking a lot about Lilly Feld," Olivia continued. "Remember her?"

"Of course I do," Wayne commented. "She was the young woman whose remains were found in the swamp. I've been following all aspects of the case closely."

Olivia was grateful for that. "I can't help wonder if there's a connection between Lilly's case and Amanda's. They'd never discovered what really happened to Lilly, either. And for a long time there wasn't much publicity about her."

"No, there wasn't," agreed Wayne. "That's often the way. Unless victims have friends and family behind them, or unless someone keeps pushing for the case to be solved, it's easy to let it fall through the cracks. The police are incredibly overloaded. They can't focus on everyone."

"That's awful," Olivia remarked.

"Yes, it is," Wayne said. "That's why I'm involved with restorative justice. We look after everyone, rich or poor, a powerful figure or a lost runaway with no place to call home."

Olivia felt her heart go out to Wayne. "That's beautiful," she whispered.

"So, if you have even the least bit of doubt, keep on the case," Wayne added.

Olivia had been planning to do that anyway, but Wayne's words gave her the added incentive. "Thank you so much," she murmured.

"So, what's your next step?" asked Wayne.

"Frank seems to know a lot about Lilly Feld," Olivia remarked, thinking out loud now. "He's the tour guide who was actually on the boat with Amanda when she disappeared. He's a cousin of Jack, the guy who owns the tour company."

"Jack's the one who got a big bonus for taking special care of Amanda?" Wayne checked.

"That's right, Jack Healey. You got it," said Olivia.

"How come Frank knows a lot about Lilly?" Wayne sounded intrigued.

"That's a good question," said Olivia. "He mentioned that he helps lost, runaway girls."

"Helps them how?" Wayne bristled. "This is important information."

"I know it is," said Olivia. "So, Frank's the next one I'm going to talk to."

"Go for it," Wayne encouraged, "but please, also stay in touch with me. Are you off the case with the police officially yet?"

"They didn't say that exactly," said Olivia.

"Okay, then do what you have to, fast," said Wayne. "You'll still have backup from them right now. It won't last forever."

*

Olivia called Frank immediately and strangely enough, he agreed to meet her down near the pier, where they'd met the last time.

128

"I'm glad you called," Frank said, to Olivia's amazement.

"Why?" she asked.

"Because my Uncle Jack is innocent and they have no right to take him in," said Frank.

"Can we talk about it in person when I meet you there?" asked Olivia.

"Absolutely," said Frank, in a hushed tone. "We can talk about anything you want this time."

It only took Olivia a little while to get down to that restaurant where she'd met Frank before. Even though the day had turned cloudy and windy, it was good being near the water again. Olivia felt invigorated just smelling the fresh, salty air. When she arrived, Frank wasn't there yet.

Olivia sat on a stool, looking out at the water, wondering what would actually come of their meeting this time. Was she pushing too hard, hoping against hope? Was Weston right when he said she didn't know how to let go?

Whether or not he was right, Olivia knew she had to try just one last time! She couldn't live with herself if she didn't.

In a few minutes Frank arrived with a narrow red scarf tied around his neck, looking eager to see Olivia. He rushed over, pulled out the stool beside her, and sat down on it promptly.

"I'm glad you're here," he said in a scruffy tone. "I'm glad you're not giving up and following like a stupid sheep."

Olivia's ears perked up.

"They're hauling my uncle in for no reason," Frank continued bitterly. "Uncle Jack is a good person. He didn't do a thing to Amanda. Her husband sent him the money to make sure his wife had a very good time. I know that for a fact because Jack gave some of the money to me, too."

"I know he did," breathed Olivia. She'd heard all this before.

"It was a tip, that's all. No big deal." Frank turned to Olivia swiftly. "Is that why you wanted to talk to me?"

"No, it isn't," she replied. "Frankly, I don't think your uncle has anything to do with this, either."

At that Frank took a deep breath. "Thank God," he muttered, throwing Olivia a grateful glance.

"I want to talk to you about something else." Olivia looked out at the wavy ocean for a second. "Tell me more about Lilly Feld."

"Who?" Frank was thrown off.

"The runaway girl they found in the swamp," said Olivia.

"Oh yeah, her!" Frank was on it. "What do you want to know about her?"

"You said you look after these lost girls," Olivia muttered. "Tell me more about that."

"Hell," Frank wavered, "I'm no knight in shining armor or anything like that. I just see them swarming all over the place and warn them to get off the streets and go back where they came from. Here and there I give them some money or buy tickets for them back home."

Olivia was moved. "Why do you do that?"

"Why not?" answered Frank. "You see a lot of them down here where I work at night. These are young kids who got derailed. Maybe they had a fight with their families they couldn't fix. Or they got caught up with drugs and alcohol. They don't deserve a life on the streets, do they?"

"No, of course they don't," breathed Olivia. "Did you talk much to Lilly Feld?"

"A little bit," said Frank. "She was sweet, too. I warned her to get off the streets and out of Key Largo. I told her there's a halfway house for sex offenders, not so far from here. Some of them get hold of young ladies."

A long chill went up and down Olivia's spine. "What did Lilly say?"

"She was high as a kite most of the time, so I don't know if she could even hear me," said Frank.

Olivia felt terrified for her. "Why haven't I heard more about the halfway house?" she asked nervously.

"No one likes to talk about it," Frank muttered. "It's bad for the tourist business. Besides, these guys are supposed to be locked up there and monitored carefully."

"Are they?" asked Olivia.

"I don't know." Frank shrugged, "I guess. But things happen too, don't they? Some of these pervs are crafty. They get loose from time to time."

"Of course they do," said Olivia. "You think one of them got Lilly?"

"Hell, how do I know?" Frank twisted on his stool. "The halfway house is fifty miles away from the swamp, so probably not."

But probably not wasn't good enough. Olivia had to know for sure.

"Anything else, Frank? You've got to tell me." Olivia's heart was beating faster now.

"That's all I know. I swear it. I talked to Lilly a few times and the next thing I heard her remains were found in the swamp."

Olivia was crestfallen. "Thanks, Frank," she said, deciding to return to the police and go over what she'd found out with them.

"Thank you for talking to me." Frank swiveled toward Olivia on the stool. "And please put a good word in for my Uncle Jack."

"I definitely will," said Olivia. "They can't hold him without solid evidence anyway, can they?"

Frank sneered. "They can do anything they damn want to," he said. "The most important thing to them is to see the case closed."

*

Before going to the police station, Olivia went back to her room to research that halfway house, who lived there, and what went on. She had to go back to the police armed with facts and figures. Then they would have no choice but to take her seriously.

As Olivia scrolled along on the computer, one article after another came up about the place. It was called Raynaud Tower and was located on the edge of a lake, down a long, winding road. Public access to it was cut off. The articles said that it was almost impossible to get in or out. To Olivia's dismay, the worst sex offenders in the state of Florida were shipped there to be monitored carefully, or in some cases rehabilitated. Some stayed for years. For others it was a short stint.

Once she'd gathered the facts, Olivia put a call in to Mike to let him know she was on her way over. Instead, Weston picked up.

"I'm coming over in a little while," Olivia announced.

"For what?" asked Weston, put out.

"I have more information that I want to talk to you about," Olivia answered sharply.

"Oh, come on now, give it a break." Weston sounded exhausted. This was obviously the last thing he wanted to deal with now.

"I can't give it a break until Amanda is found," Olivia shot back. "There's one more piece that has to be investigated."

"There's always one more piece," Weston exclaimed. "Olivia, you're gonna get a weird reputation in the business if you carry on like this. No one's gonna want to work with an obsessed person. It's time you faced reality."

"Whose reality do I have to face?" Olivia answered hotly. "I said I have information we haven't focused on yet. I'm doing my job. You hired me."

Weston relented. "All right, come down if you have to, but only for a few minutes. We're closing things up."

*

Olivia immediately hightailed it down to the station, carrying the articles about Raynaud Tower neatly folded in her briefcase. Nothing was wrong with obsession, she thought, if it has a good outcome. Weston could call her obsessed now all he liked, but if she found Amanda, his tune would change. Suddenly he'd start calling her a heroine. It didn't matter what he called her, though. What mattered to Olivia was doing what she felt was right.

Both Mike and Weston were waiting for her when she arrived. And both seemed irritated.

"What's up, Olivia?" Mike was the first to speak.

"I'd like you to pull up the records of all felons within one hundred miles," Olivia started.

Mike was amazed. "Why?" asked.

"I have reason to believe there's a felon on the loose." Olivia stretched the truth a bit.

"Who told you that?" Mike was getting jittery now.

"I just spoke to Frank." Olivia tried to sound authoritative.

"Frank's a wild card," Weston interrupted. "He always was and he always will be."

"Yeah, but he's got all kinds of weird connections." Mike became uneasy now.

"Frank said there's a halfway house fifty miles away for the worst sex offenders in Florida," Olivia announced.

Mike and Weston threw each other a strained glance.

"Yeah, so what?" Weston jumped in. "That place is fifty miles away. Basic access to it from here is through dangerous swampland filled with reptiles and snakes. You think a predator is going to swim here through that to nab a victim?"

"Not necessarily swim," said Olivia.

"Besides, the sexual predators there are guarded and under careful control," Mike added. "We ruled out the possibility that someone from that place is involved in the case at the very beginning."

"I still want the name of felons who've been freed within one hundred miles, anyway." Olivia was playing for time.

"You think one of them got hold of Amanda?" Weston sneered. "You plan to interview every one of them?" Weston was trying to undermine her request, to make it seem foolish.

"I'm particularly interested in the felons from that halfway house," Olivia replied.

"I told you, we ruled it out already." Mike wasn't going along with any of this either.

"We don't have time for something like this," Weston added. "It's a crazy detour."

"Then I'm going to visit the halfway house myself," Olivia replied.

Mike became forceful. "Olivia, the case is closed. We don't really need you on it anymore," he said.

"Just cut me some slack," Olivia suddenly pleaded. "Let me do this one last thing."

Mike and Weston looked at each other once again.

"Otherwise, I can't leave the case behind," Olivia continued. "Just this. Get me access to the halfway house. Please! Then I'll call it a day and leave."

"You're sure this is the last thing?" asked Weston.

Olivia nodded. "Yes, please. Just cut me some slack."

*

After Olivia left the station, the clouds had darkened, as they always did before a thunderstorm storm was about to hit. She'd have to wait out the storm before going down to the halfway house. There was no way she could go there alone, though. And she didn't want to go with Weston, either.

Olivia quickly put a call in to Wayne as she headed back to her hotel.

"I need your help, Wayne," she said the moment he picked up the phone.

"What's wrong?" Wayne was right on it.

"There's a halfway house for sexual predators about fifty miles down from the swamp. I've got to go and speak to the guys there."

"Whew," Wayne breathed over the phone. "That's quite a find."

"I can't go there alone," Olivia continued.

"Of course not," he exclaimed. "Don't you dare."

"Can you come up and go with me?" The words flew out of Olivia's mouth.

"Absolutely," Wayne replied without hesitation. "I'll be up there on the next flight."

CHAPTER TWENTY ONE

Olivia waited for Wayne to arrive in Key Largo, while Mike and Weston made official arrangements for her to go to the halfway house and speak to the director, Paul McKarnick. The plan was that she and Wayne would go part of the way with a tour guide on an open boat through the swamp. After that they'd make the rest of the way through back roads. A special Jeep would be waiting for them. When Olivia asked if that was the only route to get there, Mike was close-mouthed.

"It's the best route," he finally mumbled.

"But is it the only one?" asked Olivia.

"It's the one you're going on with Wayne, so be thankful for it," Mike added. "You'll be

coming back a different way. Don't worry about it." Obviously Mike didn't want to let Olivia

know the exact route back. He didn't want her going to the halfway house again on her own. Mike was also relieved Wayne was going with her.

"By the time Wayne arrives," Mike continued now, "we'll have all the arrangements ready to go."

After Mike hung up Olivia waited at her hotel both for Wayne to arrive and to receive word from Mike. As she waited Olivia realized that this was the last leg of the journey. If they didn't find anything at the halfway house, she'd have to return to Key West empty-handed, a failure. That wasn't the only reason Olivia was continuing the search. She wasn't really fully convinced that Tye was to blame for Amanda's disappearance. True, he said he'd planned to kill her and the cops had been forced to hold him. But Tye had also said then that it was a crazy plan and he never would have done it. And he did buy her that engagement ring. One second Tye was filled with vengeance, the next second he wanted to start all over again. Beyond that, they never located Amanda. Olivia kept dwelling on the fact that there was no definitive evidence that she was dead. What if Amanda were hiding somewhere, still alive, desperate to be found?

Olivia realized it was inevitable that some cases would come to a dead end. But it shook her deeply, nevertheless. It also made her realize how even one passing fact, or comment, could turn things around in a flash.

When Olivia finally heard a knock on her door, she jumped up. It had to be Wayne and she was both excited and nervous to see him again. And to make the journey with him through the swamp.

Olivia opened the door quickly. Wayne stood there, looking strong and determined. His full sandy hair was brushed back and his clear eyes looked at her intently. Olivia hadn't fully noticed how attractive he was before.

"You got here in no time at all," she murmured.

"I heard all the arrangements for the trip are ready. We're set to go," Wayne replied as he walked in.

"How do you know that?"

"Mike called and told me," Wayne replied.

Olivia was a bit put out. "I was waiting for him to let me know that," she murmured.

"Don't take offense," said Wayne. "I've known Mike awhile, and no matter what they say, it's still a bit of an old boys' club down here. Mike actually has a lot of respect for you. He mentioned a few times what a great job you've done."

"Thanks," said Olivia.

"That's why they're fulfilling your request and making all these arrangements for us to go to the halfway house."

It was good to hear that. Olivia was grateful that Wayne made it so clear. "We have quite a trip up ahead of us," she commented.

"I'm ready if you are." Wayne looked at her and smiled. "This is an important part of the search."

*

It was actually wonderful sitting beside Wayne on the open boat sloshing through the choppy waters. They could easily see the alligators spread out on rocks and hear the wild birds calling to each other, during the late afternoon.

"You're a brave woman, Olivia," Wayne said as he looked out at the surroundings in awe. "This place is gorgeous, but treacherous also."

"Amanda was brave as well, don't you think?" asked Olivia.

"She had to be," Wayne agreed. "This is incredible country to be traveling through. It's wild, untrammeled. It lures you in."

"What did Amanda really want here?" Olivia asked, looking around at the tangled trees and wild grass.

"Once we know that, we'll find out what happened to her," Wayne replied.

"Why would she venture into this kind of terrain and risk her life when she was three months pregnant?" Olivia went on. "It's not normal."

"Doesn't make sense, does it?" Wayne replied.

"Her friends said Amanda was excited to have the baby, too," Olivia went on.

"She may not have sensed danger," Wayne suggested. "Some people don't. She may have been so deeply taken by the beauty that she didn't see what was crawling right under her feet. She had no idea what could happen to her."

That was a kind way of putting it, and Olivia was moved by Wayne's response.

"Amanda also had no idea that her husband was planning to kill her," Olivia went on.

Wayne grew silent.

"She had no idea that he'd found out not only about the pregnancy but that the child didn't belong to him," Olivia added.

"That could cause lots of guys to go crazy," Wayne agreed. "How was Tye planning to kill her, exactly?"

"He didn't say. When the police pressed he backtracked, kept saying it was just a crazy idea. He said he never would have done it. It was just a passing thought."

"But he still planned it out." Wayne didn't let go. "That's going further than most. A thought is one thing, a plan is another. And on top of it, he sent that bonus to Jack."

"There's no denying that." Olivia nodded.

Wayne went over the possibilities carefully. "Could Tye have arranged for someone to be there when Amanda got off the tour boat? He knew she wanted to go further. Jack knew it too. Jack even instructed Frank to stop and let Amanda out."

"It's true, Tye could have arranged it," Olivia agreed. "But still, I don't think so."

"Why not?" asked Wayne.

"Because he also bought her a diamond ring," said Olivia. "They obviously had a love-hate relationship going on."

"And what if the hate won?" Wayne was relentless. "What if the entire trip down here was fueled for him by vengeance?"

"That's the conclusion the police came to, as well," said Olivia.

"So why don't you agree?" Wayne really wanted a clear answer.

"Because of Lilly Feld," Olivia remarked. "How could it be a coincidence that she was found at the exact the spot Amanda disappeared in?"

Wayne listened deeply. "Maybe it is coincidence and maybe not," he remarked. "It's certainly worth further investigation."

Olivia was relieved. At least Wayne was willing to take all possibilities into consideration. She liked that about him, very much.

"What do you know about this halfway house, Wayne?" Olivia asked then.

"I just know it's here, everyone knows that. I don't recall hearing about it causing any trouble in the community," Wayne replied, as the boat turned toward the edge of the swamp to let them out and onto the jungle Jeep that was waiting.

The ride on the Jeep through the tall grass and weeds was bumpy, but it was good to be on dry land. As the vehicle made its way doggedly, it shook Olivia and Wayne into one another and then back away once again. Wayne laughed and Olivia smiled as the Jeep jogged along. Soon they would arrive at their destination, the halfway house. She couldn't wait for that.

*

Raynaud Tower was deeply hidden back at the end of a road, surrounded by trees, bushes, and ponds which looked like small moats around it. After they got out of the Jeep Olivia and Wayne walked up a very narrow trail to the entrance of the halfway house. The trip had taken awhile and the light of the day was starting to fade. As they walked over jagged rocks, Olivia wanted to reach out and hold Wayne's arm for balance. She stopped herself from doing it, naturally. This was a professional expedition and Olivia had no intention of turning it into anything else.

To Olivia's surprise, a man with a straw hat and khakis stood outside the entrance, waiting for them. She wondered how he knew just when they would be arriving.

"Paul McKarnick, here," he said and looked them over carefully as Olivia and Wayne approached. Paul was in his late forties, unshaven with watery blue eyes and a ruddy complexion. Their arrival seemed to be a big deal. He was obviously not used to receiving visitors.

"Thanks for having us," Wayne started.

Paul nodded gruffly, looking mostly at Olivia, though. "We don't usually have women visiting," he remarked.

Olivia understood. It had to be jarring for him to see her here.

"Olivia is the head detective on the case," Wayne explained instantly. "She's terrific at what she does."

Paul raised his eyebrows and looked Olivia over again carefully. "Pretty young to be doing something like this," he spoke in a hoarse tone.

"It's not about age," Wayne jumped in again, "it's about getting the job done. And Olivia really does it."

"Yeah, I guess so." Paul rubbed his scruffy face. "So I guess I have to invite the two of you in," he went on. "Come in."

Paul went up ahead of them, pulled open a narrow door, and they all entered the main lobby of the building. It was half dark inside and oddly stuffy, with a few men wandering in and out. Despite herself Olivia felt uneasy.

"We have full-time residents here and some who only stay a shorter time," Paul began explaining.

Wayne nodded, looking around.

"Do you want a tour of the place?" asked Paul.

"That would be terrific," said Olivia, wondering who was here hiding here and what she would find. "We'd also like to talk not only to you, but to some of the residents."

"What for?" Paul frowned, his face getting red.

"We need to find out whatever we can that will possibly help us locate the woman who went missing," Olivia replied.

"Which woman?" Paul's eyes flared. Obviously he was aware that two women had recently disappeared.

"Both of them," said Olivia.

"Wait a minute, this is going too far." Now Paul was obviously nervous.

"It's okay, it's okay." Wayne tried to settle him down. "Olivia's thinking there could be a connection between Lilly and Amanda's disappearance."

Paul calmed a bit. "Yeah, anything's possible, isn't it? But what the hell do we have to do with any of it?"

"No one's blaming you or your operation," Wayne replied. "We just want to talk to the people here and find out if they know anything at all. Who knows? Maybe something irregular happened."

Paul grinned. "Everything's irregular here, in case you hadn't noticed. Don't know what you think you're going to find out from these fellas. Some are holed up here and don't get out, except a few times a year. Others go home to sleep every night and report back in the morning. They all wear tracing anklets on them all the time.

Some get rehabilitation, others are done with that. Still, they can't leave. If we let some loose, they'll offend again. They're not bad dudes, they just can't help it. We take good care of them."

Olivia was impressed with Paul's attitude. He was being protective of the men who lived here, didn't want his smooth operation to be shaken up.

"I look forward to talking with them," Wayne responded in a muted tone.

"You'll get all kinds of reports from the guys," Paul continued. "Some think this place worse than jail. Others are relieved to be here, away from the lousy world."

Whatever Paul said about it, Raynaud Tower felt like a last-ditch stop to Olivia. Especially for long-term residents. It was as if they'd come to the end of the road and were stuck there with each other.

"I want to talk to the residents as soon as possible," Olivia remarked then.

"I tell you one thing, honey, and this is for sure." Paul shot a dark look at Olivia. "None of these guys knew your fancy Amanda. We saw her picture on the news, but how would any of them come across someone like her in their lives?"

"What about Lilly?" Wayne was quick to ask.

"Girls like Lilly are a dime a dozen." Paul scowled. "They hang around the streets and ask for trouble. But our guys are miles away from them here. That's why we keep them monitored."

Wayne nodded slowly.

"Why don't you talk to other guys floating around free, on the outside?" Paul suggested.

"We can't talk to the whole world," Wayne replied. "We have to start somewhere. Usually we go to where there's been trouble before."

"Okay, okay, come into the main room and I'll bring some of the guys to you," Paul agreed.

"Thank you," said Olivia lightly.

"Follow me, both of you," Paul said. "This is gonna be a big treat for the guys. They don't often get to see a real live woman close enough that they could touch."

Wayne flinched. "No one's touching Olivia."

"Of course not." Paul smiled oddly. "Nothing bad's gonna happen to your girl."

Olivia felt odd being called Wayne's girl, but was certainly glad he was here with her now.

CHAPTER TWENTY TWO

Paul was right. The moment Olivia and Wayne entered the lounge down the hall, some of the men stood up and started ogling her.

"What's she doing here?" a heavyset guy on the chair nearest the door asked immediately.

"We have two visitors this evening, Olivia and Wayne," Paul announced quickly over the loud TV that was on. "They'd like to talk to some of you."

"Why?" yelled out a short thin guy in the back. "We ain't done nothing! We haven't been out of here forever."

"Two women have gone missing in the swamp," Paul continued, his hoarse voice growing louder. "If anyone knows anything at all about it, this is the time to speak!"

A loud, uneasy murmur went through the room as the guys looked at one another. Most seemed baffled, a few fascinated.

"I'll bring some of you over to the side room to talk to Olivia and Wayne," Paul continued. "It'll only take a few minutes. Just answer their questions and all will be well."

Paul led Olivia and Wayne into a room on the side that had two stiff couches and an old, dusty rug covering the floor. A big window looked across a field in the back and you could actually watch the light dimming and the evening haze drifting down.

Wayne and Olivia sat on the one of the couches as a small, wiry man was led in first.

"This is Ned," Paul announced. "He knows all the fellas and gossip. He'll be good to talk to."

Ned actually seemed pleased by the attention. "How can I help?" He had a thin, piercing voice. "I've been here for three years and two months."

"We're trying to find out all we can about Raynaud Tower," Olivia began. "We also need to find out whether any of you know about the women who recently went missing in the swamp."

"What swamp? There's no swamp around here," Ned answered.

"There's one about fifty miles down," said Wayne.

"How would we know about anything that happens down there?" Ned looked at them strangely. "We spend all our time here. They call it a halfway house, but that's pure crap. Most of us stay here full time. Some get out only to sleep and then come right back. Most of us work on the grounds, play cards, smoke, and talk about the rotten deal life handed us." Ned spoke fast. "Maybe some of us heard about those ladies on the news, but you don't hear much talk about it."

"Why not?" asked Olivia.

"Everyone here's gotten into big trouble. We've all been burnt," Ned answered. "You think we want to think about stuff like that and remember it night and day? We don't."

"Some of you guys are getting rehabilitation, aren't you?" Wayne asked then.

At that Ned smiled. "Yeah, that's what they call it. I tried it myself once. It's a big joke, doesn't amount to anything."

Olivia wondered what had happened in Ned's life and what his rehabilitation was like, but didn't dare ask. She had to stay focused upon Amanda and Lilly, couldn't go off on tangents, no matter how interesting.

"Is there anyone here who might have been down in the swamp where these ladies went missing?" Olivia asked.

"If there was, I don't know nothing about it," Ned insisted. "I wish I did but I don't."

Olivia believed him.

"Talk to the next guy who's coming in, Marvin. He's smarter than me and if something's happening, Marvin's usually heard about it."

"Great," said Olivia, "send Marvin in!"

Marvin was younger than Ned, looked almost like a newcomer here. His hands shook at his sides and he sat down abruptly.

"I didn't mean to hurt anyone," Marvin started before they had a chance to say a word.

Olivia felt bad for him. "We're not here about your case," she quickly said.

"They blame me for everything anyway now," Marvin went on.

"Who blames you for what?" asked Wayne, disturbed.

"The minute they hear a kid got killed, they come back here and grill me again." Marvin sounded as if he were about to break down. "It's always me."

"Sorry to hear that," said Wayne.

"That's not why we're here now," Olivia went on.

Marvin stopped a second and tried to listen. "You're not here because of that?"

"Not at all," Olivia repeated. "Two women went missing fifty miles down in the swamp. We just wondered if you'd heard about it?"

Marvin looked dazed, trying hard to remember. "I think I saw something about it on TV," he finally replied.

"Did you hear any of the guys here talking about it?" Wayne chimed in. "Anybody have any possible ideas about how it happened?"

Marvin looked sadly at Wayne. "Most of the guys don't talk to me," he said then. "Three of the kids I got involved with ended up dead. When they find that out, no one has another word to say. I'm the lowest of the lowest, the worst of the worst."

"Sorry to hear that, Marvin," Wayne said and meant it.

"Yeah, me, too, very sorry," said Marvin, standing up to go. "I have nothing to add, ever." He started walking out of the room.

Olivia and Wayne looked at each other a bit hopelessly then. "This is a fishing expedition," said Olivia.

"Yes, it is. That's okay," said Wayne. "Let's keep at it anyway. Someone might have a different slant."

"Sal's coming in next," Paul called in then through the door as a large, good-looking guy wearing jeans entered.

"Tell me what you need and I'll give you the answer," Sal said immediately, straddling the chair. "Then one hand washes another. I help you and you help me get out!" Sal flashed them a winning smile.

Olivia couldn't help but smile back. "I wish we could, Sal," she started, "but it doesn't work like that."

"It could if you wanted, though, couldn't it?" Sal was a charmer. Was that how he'd caught his prey?

"I'm an independent detective on the case," said Olivia. "Getting you out of here is way beyond my purview."

Sal seemed to like Olivia and grinned. "Okay, tell me what you need and I'll help you anyway. Heck, I'll do anything for a pretty face."

Olivia wondered what Sal had done to land here, wished she could have been helpful to him in some way.

Wayne picked up the ball quickly. "You heard about the two women who went missing in the swamp?" he started.

"Sure did," said Sal, rubbing his hands on this thighs. "Stupid to be there, both of them. They had to be looking for trouble."

"Definitely a dangerous place," Wayne agreed.

"That's for sure," said Sal. "So what can I do?"

"Do you know anyone at all here who might have been in that area when they disappeared?" asked Wayne.

"That's quite a question!" Sal replied.

"And we need an answer badly," said Wayne.

Sal paused, seemed to be thinking it over.

"I work with the restorative justice project." Wayne nudged him forward. "If there's any chance you're innocent, maybe I can help."

Sal looked over at him, startled. "I'm not innocent," he replied bluntly. "I'm sorry as hell for what I did, but I'm not innocent. If I got out everyone says I'd do it again. I don't know if it's true. I'd try not to, sure, but I don't know."

Olivia was moved by the power of Sal's honesty.

"I'll help you anyhow," Sal suddenly blurted out. "Listen, there's a guy in this place, Raul, who has a fishing shack somewhere in those parts. It's not in the swamp exactly, it's between the swamp and this place. You get there by Jeep. He's also got an old Jeep parked in the back."

"How do you know this?" Wayne was all over it.

"Raul talks about his shack a lot," Sal said. "He's just here for rehab, so he's free to come and go more than most. Sometimes he goes for too long though. Lots of times I don't see him returning until noon."

"Did you tell the authorities?" Olivia was startled.

"It's an unspoken law here that nobody snitches on each other here," said Sal. "If you do there's hell to pay."

"Are you snitching now?" asked Wayne.

"No, this is something else," Sal corrected him. "I'm not snitching! I'm helping with an investigation. And maybe someday someone will help me, too."

Wayne looked troubled. "Tell us more, please."

"Raul's a funny guy," Sal went on. "When I ask him what he does during the mornings, he just smiles, stretches, and says, freedom is sweet, brother. Too bad you don't have it."

"Seems like a fair enough thing to say," said Olivia.

"Maybe on the surface it is," agreed Sal. "But when I noticed a few days he didn't come back until late in the afternoon I asked him where he was. He told me to go to hell, said he comes and goes as he likes. If I have a problem with that, drop dead."

"He didn't want you on all over him," Wayne suggested.

"Maybe," Sal agreed. "But nobody's allowed to come and go like that. This guy is slippery. He's a fisherman and hunter, but now he's also been convicted of a sex crime."

"How come they slack off where Raul's concerned?" Olivia was frightened.

"A few always get through the cracks, don't they?" said Sal. "The sneaky ones. And his attitude grates me. You came here asking if I knew something fishy, so I had to tell you about him."

"Yes, you did," said Olivia.

"Well, that makes me happy." Sal smiled at her again.

"Can you tell us exactly where his fishing shack is?" Wayne interrupted.

"I sure can," said Sal. "I know the exact route too. You take the long road behind our place, go up and down a few hills and follow it to the very end."

*

After the interviews were over Olivia and Wayne had a few minutes in the room together alone.

"We've got to get right to Raul's fishing shack," was the first thing Olivia said.

"It wouldn't hurt," Wayne agreed, slowing down the urgency. "We can go there some time tomorrow."

"No." Olivia felt wired. "There's no time to wait. Let's go tonight."

"It's impossible, we can't get there tonight," Wayne said. "And there's a Jeep waiting outside to take us back to Key Largo now."

"Please, Wayne," Olivia said in a strong tone. "I can't go back now. Something tells me we have to get to that hut, as soon as possible!"

"We can't, it's dark out now." Wayne wouldn't go along with it. "There's low visibility. And there's a very far-off chance we'll find anything there at all."

"It's all we have left, though," said Olivia.

Wayne took a deep breath. "I have work to do early in the morning tomorrow," he said. "There are a few conference calls to be on. We can go after that in the afternoon. That's the best I can do for now."

"What choice do I have?" Olivia breathed.

"None at all," said Wayne. "Let's go now, the Jeep's waiting for us. We'll get to our hotels, get a good sleep, and come back to the hut tomorrow."

CHAPTER TWENTY THREE

Back in her hotel and exhausted, Olivia went right to bed. She'd done enough for one day, couldn't even think about it anymore now. Even though she fell asleep immediately, Olivia kept tossing and turning in her sleep. The image of the fishing hut wouldn't leave her. It called to her, telling her to come right now. Startled, Olivia awoke once again, sat up, and shivered. She was also disturbed by the notion of Raul coming and going freely. Why wasn't he being carefully monitored? How had he managed to pull that off? Olivia not only wanted to check the fishing hut, but hopefully run into him as well.

After a sleepless night, she got out of bed at the crack of dawn. Even before ordering breakfast in, she immediately texted Mike and Weston information about her visit.

This is urgent, Olivia texted. *I must go to the hut immediately. No choice about it.*

A text came back from Weston instantly. *Fine, but don't go alone. Wait for Wayne to accompany you.*

Wayne's tied up all morning, Olivia texted back.

I can go there with you later on, Weston texted back.

Olivia's heart started pounding. It wasn't possible to wait until later.

I can't wait, she texted back to Weston.

You have to, Weston replied. *It's a long shot anyway, at best.*

It's not a long shot, it's the only shot, Olivia replied.

After ordering a quick breakfast up to her room, Olivia decided not to waste any more time. There were plenty of Jeep drivers to hire who could take her there immediately. She just needed exact directions. Olivia decided to put a quick call in to Frank to tell her exactly how to get where she was going. Frank had said he'd help her in any way he could. This was his opportunity.

Frank picked up the phone the moment Olivia called. "I expected to hear from you sooner or later," he started. "Why now?"

"There's a fishing hut I've got to get to immediately," Olivia breathed. "It's between the swamp and the halfway house."

She could feel Frank listening intently on the other end. "Did you go to the halfway house?"

"Yes, I did," said Olivia. "Yesterday."

"Good for you," said Frank. "That's what I call guts."

"Can you take me to the fishing hut?" Olivia continued.

"Take you there when, today?" Frank sounded alarmed.

"Not today, this morning! Right now!" Olivia responded.

"Nothing like giving a guy plenty of notice," Frank replied.

"Can you?"

"No, not right away." Frank scraped his throat. "What's the big emergency?"

"I spoke to the guys at the halfway house," Olivia blurted out, "and they told me about this place."

"There are lots of huts like that sprinkled in that area," said Frank. "What's the big deal?"

Olivia paused a moment before answering. It was a big deal and she knew it, but she couldn't say why.

"I need to get there right away," she repeated.

"I know the area you're talking about and I can give you directions to get there," said Frank. "That's the best I can do for now."

"Give me the directions then," said Olivia, whipping out a little pad.

As Frank dictated directions carefully, Olivia wrote them down. "Make sure you take that route and not another," he finished up. "There are all kinds of winding roads down there that lead to dead ends."

"Can a driver get me to the hut exactly?" asked Olivia then.

Frank paused. "There are plenty of Jeep drivers you can hire to take you to the vicinity, but once you get there, you're on your own. Then you take a walking path which will bring you straight to the hut."

"Thanks," said Olivia.

"Who's accompanying you?" Frank sounded on edge.

"The Jeep driver," said Olivia.

"I mean is somebody going with you all the way to the shack?"

"I'll take the Jeep driver with me all the way," Olivia answered.

"And what if he doesn't want to go?" Frank laughed.

"Why wouldn't he?" asked Olivia.

"Depends who you get," Frank replied.

"Listen, thanks for the help," Olivia said then.

"Thank you for putting a good word in for Jack," said Frank.

Frank hung up the phone and Olivia was pleased to have specific directions. It would be a mistake to wait until afternoon.

She decided to immediately hire a Jeep driver and go there on her own.

*

Olivia sat in the back of the Jeep as the driver took her through curvy roads that ran behind the glades and around it. The day was especially humid, with all kinds of insects hitting the roof of the vehicle. Rain was coming soon and she felt it. Olivia had given the driver exact directions and he'd said he was familiar with the place. She hadn't asked him yet if he would accompany her to Raul's hut, but couldn't imagine any reason that he'd say no.

As they pushed along through the thick air, Olivia was glad she left early. Thunderstorms were rumbling up ahead. This had to be the best time to get into the shack and look around. Olivia felt that she'd definitely find something there that would lead her to Amanda.

As they got closer the Jeep began slowing down.

"Almost there," the driver called out to her.

"Great," said Olivia, surprised they'd gotten here so quickly.

The Jeep came to a sudden halt then, bumping her against the side.

"Okay, all out," he called as Olivia looked around at where she'd landed.

"Where are we, exactly?" she asked. There was nothing in sight except clusters of trees. "Where are the walking paths?"

The driver shrugged. Then he pointed to the paper she'd given him. "This is where you said you wanted to go," he declared. "I followed the directions exactly."

Frank had seemed so certain about the directions that Olivia never questioned the route he'd sent her on.

"Okay, get out of the Jeep now," the driver repeated.

"Will you come with me up the trail to the hut?" asked Olivia.

"What trail?" The driver looked at her as though she were crazy. "What hut?"

"I've got to follow a walking trail that ends at a fishing hut," Olivia repeated.

The driver squinted his eyes and looked around. "You'll get there fine yourself. Just go straight ahead."

"Can you come with me?" Olivia repeated.

"Not right now, I've got another job. I'll come back for you later, if you want me to. Just give me a call. Shoot me a text."

Olivia was taken aback. "It won't take long," she asked one more time.

"I can't, I'm sorry," he repeated, quickly hopping into the Jeep and taking off.

*

Startled and standing there alone, Olivia began walking slowly, looking for the traces of a trail to walk on. Instead she found pockets of earth dug up, with soil scattered flatly around them. Could those be the walking trails Sal had mentioned? Olivia wondered as she walked further onward in the enclosure, away from the spot she'd arrived at. Frank had said there were many shacks in the area, but Olivia didn't see any of them at all. Was the tall grass hiding them from her? As the heat grew stronger and the air more humid, Olivia walked around and around in circles. She was lost, she realized in a moment of distress. The driver must have let her out at the wrong enclosure. Or had Frank had given her the wrong directions purposely? Did he know Raul? Was he going to contact him and warn him that Olivia was on her way?

Olivia knew that she couldn't let her imagination run wild, especially in a situation like this. It could only make things worse, drive her crazy, take her entirely off course. She grabbed her phone to put in a call to Wayne. To her horror, her phone was dead. No reception out here probably.

Olivia sat down on an old log that was a few feet ahead of her and put her head in her hands. At least she'd told Weston she was headed out here. But would he know just where to find her? The morning was passing and the sun growing hotter overhead.

Olivia sat there for a while, growing upset and dizzy, when she suddenly heard the wheels of a vehicle in the distance coming closer.

Thank God, she thought as she jumped up, running to the road the Jeep had arrived on. She would wave this vehicle down, ask for help, and get new directions.

As she stood there in the middle of the road, a Jeep in the distance approached. Olivia began waving her hands fervently as it got closer and slowed down.

To her total relief and delight, Wayne jumped out of the Jeep instantly.

"Wayne!" Olivia called out joyfully, wanting to throw her arms around him.

"What are you doing here alone? You've got to be crazy!" Wayne was not only distressed, but angry. "What kind of stunt are you pulling?"

Olivia was taken aback. "It's not a stunt, I came here with a Jeep driver. I thought he'd go all the way with me to the fishing hut."

"That's nuts," Wayne insisted. "It shows poor judgment, Olivia."

"Frank gave me the directions," she went on. "He said there were plenty of walking paths here and huts were sprinkled all over."

"He was wrong, wasn't he?" Wayne looked around. "I don't see any huts here."

"Somewhere close by though, I'm sure of it," Olivia pleaded.

"You've gone off the deep end," Wayne uttered. "That can happen to some of us, it's dangerous. It happens when we think a case is over and time is running out. Then the incredible craving to find the victim kicks in and intensifies, and we lose good judgment."

Olivia listened to Wayne, enrapt. "Yes," she murmured, feeling as though that's what had happened to her.

Wayne calmed down then and put his arms around her shoulders. "Thank God I found you when I did," he said.

"Thank God," Olivia agreed as the two of them gazed at each other.

"Okay, let's get back in the Jeep now and continue forward," Wayne said. "There's another road parallel to this one. It leads to where we want to go. The driver will take us there and then, together, we'll get out and take the walking path straight to Raul's hut. The driver will stay back and wait for us to return."

Wayne had every detail figured out. Olivia was enormously grateful not only that he found her, but that he knew exactly how to proceed.

CHAPTER TWENTY FOUR

Olivia and Wayne went back into the Jeep and the driver started it up. He drove straight ahead for a short while, then swerved onto a different road that dipped down quickly and proceeded between tall marsh grass, which blew wildly in the wind.

"Storm coming up soon," the driver announced, glancing out the window at the grass weaving.

The driver proceeded silently for about fifteen more minutes until they arrived at

the walking path Frank had mentioned.

"This is it, here you are," the driver called out.

"Okay, we get out here," said Wayne to Olivia, as he jumped out of the Jeep. "That wasn't so hard. Actually, it was easy."

Olivia followed him out of the Jeep and they stood together silently for a moment, looking at the long walking path in front of them.

"I'll wait back here for you," said the driver.

"We won't be long," Wayne answered. "Thanks."

Once out of the Jeep, Olivia stood tall and quickly regained her balance. She and Wayne quickly stepped onto the walking path, which wound a trail away from the main road through tangled bushes. Low-flying birds and insects of all kinds buzzed around them as they walked along.

The deeper they went, the darker it became, damper and more humid. Heavy clouds drifted down over the area and once again Olivia wanted to reach for Wayne's hand. She would not, though.

"We're almost there," Wayne said then, looking up ahead and pointing down the path to a small, broken down shack that looked just like the place they were aiming for. "This matches the description Sal gave us, doesn't it?"

"Yes, exactly," said Olivia.

"Okay, we'll get in and out fast, before the heavy rain starts," Wayne continued. "You were right, it was better to get here earlier."

Olivia gazed down the road at a totally nondescript structure that she wouldn't normally have even bothered to glance at.

"This is it?" she asked, disappointed.

"It's something, anyway," said Wayne. "We'll go in, look around, and see if anything's been left around there that could help. Then we'll get right back into the Jeep before the rain starts up."

From the tone of his voice, Olivia felt as if Wayne might simply be going along so she could finally accept the case was over.

Step by step they continued on toward the cabin when a low, screeching sound came wafting toward them on the heavy air.

"What's that?" asked Olivia, startled.

"Sounds like a bird that got hurt," Wayne replied.

The screech sounded again, stronger this time, rising in pitch and intensity.

"You think the bird's trapped somewhere?" asked Olivia, agitated. "It sounds like it's in pain."

"Could be," said Wayne. "A snake could have gotten it, or a crocodile. Could be it's been caught alive, struggling to get free."

The image sent shivers over Olivia. They took another few steps and the sound increased.

"It's nearby," Olivia said then, trembling as the sound became bloodcurdling. It was so fierce it stopped the two of them in their tracks.

"Wait a minute," Wayne whispered, "what is it?"

"It's not a bird," gasped Olivia as they traced the noise straight to the shack they were headed toward.

"You're right!" Wayne looked at Olivia, alarmed. "Let's get in there immediately!"

As Olivia and Wayne ran up to the front door the sound turned to full out shrieks. They charged at the door full force together, instantly pushing it in.

In the dark Olivia immediately saw a woman huddled in the fetal position on the floor. A tall, deranged-looking man stood over her, raising his arm to her head, as if to hit her, then putting it down.

"Amanda!" Olivia yelled at the top of her lungs, shocking them both. "Is it you, Amanda? Tell me!"

Instantly, Wayne lunged at the man from behind, pulling him back away from the woman, who was sobbing hysterically.

"Don't cry, we're here, Amanda," Olivia yelled, beside herself, rushing over to her.

In the background Olivia heard the sound of Wayne and the other man pushing each other, grunting, stamping their feet on the ground.

"Get the hell off me, you bastard," the guy's heavy voice thundered.

"Put your hands behind your back." Wayne was threatening him. "I've got a gun and I'll use it."

As Olivia spun around she saw Wayne pulling his gun out.

In the next flash of a second the guy lunged at Wayne, knocking him off balance, kicking him and knocking him down. Then the guy then plunged down next to Wayne and grabbed his gun, which was lying beside him on the ground. The guy, who was big, with dark hair and a scar on his face, stood there, grinning.

Could this be Raul? Olivia wondered. Was it possible?

"Raul?" Olivia asked.

"Don't you dare say my name, bitch," the guy answered, waving the gun over his head.

"Put the gun down, Raul," Olivia ordered.

"When hell freezes over, I will," he grunted. "Nice of this fella to bring me a gun." Raul then took a step closer to Wayne and slammed the edge of the gun down on Wayne's shoulder hard.

Wayne shouted in pain as Olivia heard the slam of the steel gun hit his bones.

"Wayne, Wayne," she cried out, rushing toward him, throwing herself over him to protect him.

"Get back off me." Wayne could barely speak. "We don't both need to die."

At least he didn't shoot, though, thought Olivia, her heart beating out of her mouth, as she moved slightly away.

"That's just for starters, buddy," Raul hollered as Wayne lay there, wincing in pain. "In another second I'm killing each one of you. In fact, I've been waiting for this moment. I've been wondering how I would finish off this lousy standoff."

The woman on the floor reached her hands up over her ears and turned her head so that in the dim light, Olivia could make out that it was indeed Amanda. Her face was sweaty and terrified, streaked with days of pain and fear.

"My God, my God, Amanda," Olivia wailed. "You're alive. This is real. We found you."

"Found her only to lose her," Raul breathed heavily.

"What did she do to you?" Olivia asked him thunderstruck.

Raul guffawed. "What did this lousy world do to me? You want me to sit down and tell you? You'd be here for at least a hundred years."

"So you get back at random people?" Enraged, Olivia turned toward him with the full force of fury. "You're a coward, Raul."

Raul stopped for a second and glared at her.

Overcome by the senselessness of his actions, Olivia lost all fear of him. "Put down that gun, or it's all over," she threatened.

"You think you're going to tell me what to do?" Raul sneered and took another step toward Wayne again, kicking him hard in the thigh.

Olivia crept away from Wayne along the floor. Then she grabbed both of Raul's legs out from under him, shocking him, pulling him off balance and dragging him down hard on the ground.

As Raul hit the ground the gun in his hand fell beside him. Olivia grabbed it immediately.

The hard feel of the steel in her hands was both frightening and powerful. She had to take action fast, too, or he'd grab it back from her.

Without another moment of thought, Olivia pointed the weapon and shot Raul in one leg and then another.

His screams mixed with the blood that started pouring out onto the dank, earthen floor.

"I'll get you for this!" Raul cursed heartily. "You'll never get away from me. Not ever."

Wayne pulled himself up slowly and moved over to Olivia. "Good, good," he said, leaning on her and holding his shoulder.

With his good arm, Wayne then grabbed his phone and immediately put in a call for backup. He was hurt, but at least he could walk, thought Olivia. At least he was alive.

"Is Raul dead? Is he finished?" Amanda called in a raspy tone.

"Raul's not dead," said Olivia, shaking, "just incapacitated."

"Get him away from me, get me out of here." Amanda began to wail.

Olivia went over and put her arms around her to calm her. "It's over now, you're safe. He can't hurt you any longer," she whispered.

"He can always hurt us, he can." Amanda was beside herself. "He told me that over and over. He said I could die at any moment. It was up to him and no one else."

"It was never up to him, Amanda." Olivia spoke with a strange strength. "There's a ruler of the world who's in charge of who lives and dies."

"Get me out of here, get me away, I beg you." Amanda could not stop.

Raul, writhing in pain, looked up at both of them then, a horrible glint in his eyes.

"I let you live and I shouldn't have," he snarled at Amanda. "But I enjoyed watching you suffer day by day. It gave me strength, it gave me energy. It gave me something to live for each day."

Hearing those words, Wayne made his way over to Olivia and grabbed the gun from her.

"Where's your energy now, buddy?" Wayne aimed the gun at Raul. "What happened to all the pleasure you got from torturing her and a bunch of other people?"

A look of horrible fright came over Raul's face.

"Don't kill him, please!" Amanda cried loudly.

Wayne and Olivia stared at her, thunderstruck.

"He let me live. He didn't kill me!" Amanda couldn't stop speaking.

Wayne closed his eyes a moment.

"Let's wait for backup, Wayne," Olivia agreed. "Let the cops step in and decide Raul's fate."

*

As Olivia cradled Amanda in her arms, the cops arrived in what seemed like no time.

"It's over, it's over," Olivia kept repeating as Amanda trembled terrifically.

"Who are you? How did you find me?" Amanda whispered.

"We'll talk more later," Olivia assured her, "just rest now." This wasn't the time to ask Amanda what happened. There would be plenty of time for that later on.

The cops came in with medical backup for Amanda and hauled Raul away.

"You really missed a bullet here," a cop said to both Olivia and Wayne. "No one had any idea what was going on in this shack."

"Olivia did," said Wayne.

The cops cast Olivia an offhand glance. "It's a miracle, anyway," one of them said.

Then they looked at Amanda. "We have an ambulance coming for her," they proclaimed.

"An ambulance, why?" Amanda sat up slowly, looking around the shack. "I've been here for days and I made it through."

"Just a necessary precaution," one of the policemen said slowly. You've been through hell and back."

Amanda looked at him. She was fragile and sad after her incredible ordeal. "I'm all right, I made it," she managed to repeat.

"Yes, you did," Olivia murmured.

"I always knew I'd make it," Amanda added. "I knew it wasn't my time to die."

"That itself could have kept you alive." Olivia was amazed by Amanda's strength.

Is it true, it's over now, forever?" Amanda continued.

"It's over," Wayne answered firmly, joining them. "Raul has been taken into custody. He'll never be able to harm anyone again."

"Does Tye know what happened?" Amanda looked at both of them sadly.

"He knew you were missing," Olivia managed to say.

"Was he upset about it?" Amanda now had trouble talking.

"Yes, of course, he was upset," said Olivia.

"Maybe he was and maybe he wasn't." Amanda tossed her head back and forth.

Olivia didn't know if it was safe for the two of them to be back together now. "Time will help you understand everything," she whispered to Amanda. "Everyone will be shocked to see you, though. No one had much hope that you were still alive."

Amanda looked more and more sorrowful. "Is this is my fault?" she barely mouthed. "I really thought it was completely safe to go a little bit further into the swamp."

*

The ambulance came to take Amanda to the hospital, and Olivia and Wayne accompanied her, in the back. The doctors wanted Wayne to check into the hospital as well, and have his shoulder examined. Amanda lay on a stretcher silently, staring out the window. Olivia could only imagine what she had to be thinking about.

"We'll get in touch with Tye as soon as we return," Olivia said to her.

"No rush about that," Amanda replied quietly. "First I need time to get back to myself. Don't know if I ever will again."

*

The ambulance arrived at the hospital and Olivia waited in the lounge while Amanda and Wayne were being examined. Like Amanda, Olivia didn't feel like seeing anyone at the moment. The entire rush of events came over her with the force of a tidal wave. She needed time to step out of the current and let things quiet down. At times it was almost as if she were dreaming. It was amazing to realize that they'd found Amanda alive. Olivia had been right about continuing to search. But there were so many questions still unanswered. Would Tye be released from jail? Was he somehow complicit in what had happened to Amanda?

As Olivia sat there wondering, she saw Weston and Mike walk into the lounge and make their way right over to her.

"Dear God, are you all right?" was the first thing Mike said.

"I'm perfectly fine," said Olivia. "Wayne was the one who got hurt, not me."

"We've checked in on Wayne and his shoulder's not broken, only slightly dislocated," Mike reported. "He'll be fine in no time."

Olivia was tremendously relieved to hear that. "Good," she breathed.

"You realize that you've saved Amanda's life singlehandedly," Weston said then. "If you hadn't insisted that we continue the search, we wouldn't have."

Olivia nodded, grateful that Weston finally saw the truth. "Obsession can be good, can't it?" she added, as Weston smiled.

"It's Amanda I'm worried about, though," Olivia continued. "What will become of her now?"

"What do you mean?" asked Mike. "So far she's doing very well. Doctors say she's in shock and dehydrated, but will get over it soon."

"How's her pregnancy?" Olivia added.

"That's being checked carefully, right now," Mike offered. "No reason to think the worst."

"But should Amanda go back to Tye now? Is she really safe with him?" Olivia was thinking out loud.

"That's going to be up to Amanda, isn't it?" Weston interrupted.

Olivia was startled by his response. "Why? Are you releasing Tye from custody?" Olivia was concerned.

"Tye broke down sobbing when he heard Amanda was alive," Weston continued. "He begged us to let him see her. We haven't yet because the doctors say she needs some time to get her bearings. Amanda's a strong woman with a will to live. She'll make the right decision."

"But you could be putting her back in danger." Olivia felt flummoxed again. "How do you know there's no connection between Tye and Raul?" Olivia was still having a hard time putting it all down.

Weston continued respectfully. "We have a larger take on the picture now," he started. "The police have been questioning Raul and he's confessed to also grabbing and killing Lilly Feld."

"That's huge," breathed Olivia.

"Yes, it is," Weston agreed. "Raul's a registered sex offender. Once he got a taste of blood and seeing his victim in pain, he liked it, wanted more. That's how it happens. They get addicted to the power that comes from seeing their victims suffer. Raul was looking for another thrill and Amanda was just a random woman who drifted into his territory. When she got off the boat, it was feeding time and he was lying in wait for whoever came along. We don't see any connection whatsoever between Raul and Tye."

Olivia sighed slowly. "But Tye said he'd been planning to kill Amanda."

"Yes, he said that," Weston continued, "and we're going to have to let Amanda know what he said. When she's ready, we'll tell her. Then it's up to her to decide what to do. There's a difference between words and actions. Lots of spouses have thoughts like that at times."

Olivia's head was spinning. It would take time for her to put it all this together and she felt especially protective of Amanda right now.

Weston kneeled down then, to be closer to Olivia and talk to her face to face. "One of the roughest parts of doing this work is getting close to people and caring," he said slowly. "Then, all of a sudden the case is over and you've got to back away. What the people do in their lives then is none of your business anymore."

It was a harsh way of putting it, but Weston made his point.

"That's why I try to keep it as cool as I can," he added. "That's why I may seem tougher than I want to."

Olivia smiled despite herself. She got it. Weston was working hard to keep his heart protected from getting hurt. And he was trying to teach Olivia to do the same. He didn't want her to get hurt, or too involved, either.

"Thanks, Weston," Olivia said gratefully. "I've learned a lot on this case."

He grinned. "And there's more to come," he added. "You're all over the news now again. Everyone's talking about what a heroine you are and what a fabulous detective! The cases are going to start pouring in. I hope you're ready."

CHAPTER TWENTY FIVE

Mike and Weston left and Olivia sat silently waiting to see Wayne. She felt terrible about what happened to him, wondered if he was in pain now. She was anxious to see him again and make sure all was well.

In a short while Wayne came out, his shoulder in a sling, but smiling nevertheless.

Olivia jumped up and ran over to him. "Thank God, you're all right," she breathed.

"Better than ever." Wayne was happy to see her as well.

"I'm so sorry I got you involved in this and caused you harm." Olivia felt breathless.

"Not at all." Wayne was taken aback. "Firstly, it was an honor to be called in on the case. Secondly, I'm all right. You never caused me harm. Everyone gets a few bumps and bruises in this line of work. It's part of the game."

"I guess it is." Olivia was moved by his response.

Wayne suddenly reached out with his good arm then, pulled Olivia toward him and gave her a warm hug.

"Actually, you've been stupendous," he whispered. "You put yourself in the line of fire to save me when I was down. I'll never forget that."

Olivia had forgotten it, though. "It all happened so fast," she murmured, "it was just a natural response."

"Not natural for everyone," Wayne replied. "It says the world about who you are."

"Thanks, Wayne," Olivia said. "And thank God, we got Raul. Mike told me that he sang like a bird. They've got a full confession."

"Yes, they have." Wayne nodded, suddenly looking as though he had something on his mind. "There's so much more I want to say, too," he added.

"Please say it, go ahead," said Olivia.

Wayne seemed emotional then. "I want to make sure you realize that it was good you called me in on the case. You had to. You're incredible at this work, Olivia, but no one can do it alone."

"I realize that fully now," Olivia agreed.

"I have more to say, too." Wayne hesitated. "We'll talk more later."

"Why not now?" Olivia wanted to hear everything he had to say. "There's no reason to delay."

Wayne took a deep breath and barreled on. "It's really great working with you," he started softly.

"It's really great working with you, too," Olivia replied.

"And in case you haven't happened to notice, we're an amazing team," Wayne threw in for good measure.

"I definitely noticed that." Olivia smiled, trying to imagine what Wayne really had on his mind. It sounded as if he were leading up to something, but she was not sure what.

Wayne stepped back then and grinned at her boyishly. "You know that things at the force have been going downhill for me for a while now," he continued.

Olivia got the shivers. "Yes, I realize, you've mentioned it."

Wayne paused then, not saying anything.

"What is it, Wayne? What are you trying to tell me?" Olivia prodded him along.

Suddenly, he took the plunge. "I was thinking how great it would be to leave the force and to become partners with you," he blurted out.

"Partners in my private investigation firm?" Olivia was startled, but also thrilled at the same time.

"Yes. You're going to have much more work than you can handle very soon, anyway." Wayne didn't hold back. "There's no way you can't do it all alone."

"No, I can't," agreed Olivia. "I was just thinking that myself."

"And you won't always be working with a police force at your side." Wayne was on a roll now. "But you're always going to need ongoing backup, Olivia. We all do."

"True again," said Olivia, growing more and more excited as he spoke.

Wayne took a step closer. "Interested in joining forces?" he asked.

Olivia grinned. "More than interested, Wayne! I love the idea!"

"You do?" He looked delighted.

"Yes, I absolutely love it! And it makes perfect sense," she exclaimed.

"Well, then let's go for it." He smiled. "This is exactly what the doctor ordered. I'll leave the force and we can build the company together. O and W Private Investigators, Olivia and Wayne."

Both of them laughed at the same moment.

"It's going to work perfectly for both of us," said Wayne. "I feel it in my bones."

NO PLACE FOR MARRIAGE
(Murder in the Keys—Book #4)

"Jaden Skye creates a set of characters that are very well developed, and makes you cheer for our heroine on every page. The environment and the overall description of scenes are superb, making you feel the suspense in the air the whole time."
--Books and Movie Reviews (Roberto Mattos) (re No Place to Die)

NO PLACE FOR MARRIAGE is book #4 in a new romantic suspense series by #1 bestselling author Jaden Skye, which begins with Book #1, NO PLACE TO DIE, a free download!

When Tyron Barr, a rich, old tycoon confined to a wheelchair, is found dead at the bottom of his staircase, his stunning 32 year old wife is immediately suspect.

But she protests her innocence—and calls Olivia and Wayne in to prove it.

In a world where nothing is as it seems, a world of incredible wealth and charm, of intense greed and jealousy, loneliness and secrets, Olivia discovers, lurk behind the scenes. Perhaps just enough to murder someone.

Is the young wife playing Olivia?

Or did someone else want him dead?

NO PLACE FOR MARRIAGE is book #4 in an explosive new romantic suspense series filled with love, tragedy, heartbreak, betrayal and suspense, one that will leave you turning pages late into the night. Book #5 will be released soon.

Jaden is also author of the #1 Bestselling series MURDER IN THE CARIBBEAN, which begins with DEATH BY HONEYMOON (Book #1).

About Jaden Skye

#1 bestselling author Jaden Skye is author of the bestselling romantic suspense series CARIBBEAN MURDER, which includes 16 books (and counting), and which begins with DEATH BY HONEYMOON (Book #1).

Jaden is also author of the romance series A PERFECT STRANGER.

Jaden is also author of the new romantic suspense series MURDER IN THE KEYS, which begins with NO PLACE TO DIE (Book #1).

Jaden has always been fascinated with mystery, wrongful death, lies, deception and the power of the truth to prevail. Her romantic suspense/mystery novels feature strong female protagonists who must overcome insurmountable obstacles, and through them, she seeks to get to the very heart of the nature of justice and love. Please visit www.jadenskye.com to find links to stay in touch with Jaden via Facebook, Twitter, Goodreads, her blog, and a whole bunch of other places. Jaden loves to hear from you, so don't be shy and check back often!

Books by Jaden Skye

THE CARIBBEAN MURDER SERIES
DEATH BY HONEYMOON (Book #1)
DEATH BY DIVORCE (Book #2)
DEATH BY MARRIAGE (Book #3)
DEATH BY DESIRE (Book #4)
DEATH BY DECEIT (Book #5)
DEATH BY JEALOUSY (Book #6)
DEATH BY PROPOSAL (Book #7)
DEATH BY OBSESSION (Book #8)
DEATH BY DEVOTION (Book #9)
DEATH BY BETRAYAL (Book #10)
DEATH BY REQUEST (Book #11)
DEATH BY ENGAGEMENT (Book #12)
DEATH BY SEDUCTION (Book #13)
DEATH BY TEMPTATION (Book #14)
DEATH BY INVITATION (Book #15)
DEATH BY WEDDING (Book #16)

THE TOM'S RIVER SAGA
A PERFECT STRANGER (Book #1)

MURDER IN THE KEYS
NO PLACE TO DIE (Book #1)
NO PLACE TO VANISH (Book #2)
NO PLACE FOR VENGEANCE (Book #3)
NO PLACE FOR MARRIAGE (Book #4)

THE KILLING GAME
INVITATION TO DIE (Book #1)
INVITATION TO MADNESS (Book #2)
INVITATION TO AGONY (Book #3)

83139268R00092

Made in the USA
Lexington, KY
09 March 2018